Alpha Male

By Sheila Donald

Copyright © 2016 Sheila Donald
Published by CreateSpace Independent Publishing

The moral right of Sheila Donald to be identified as the author of this work has been asserted in accordance with the UK Copyright, Designs and Patents Act of 1988

This book is a work of fiction. All names, characters, brands and events, other than those clearly in the public domain are either the products of the author's imagination or are used fictitiously, and any similarity to real persons, living or dead, is entirely coincidental and not intended by the author
Any people depicted in cover images are models used for illustrative purposes only
Stock imagery © Shutterstock
Lyrics to 'I lift my eyes up' by kind permission of Song Solutions on behalf of Doerksen

All rights reserved. No part of this book may be reproduced, or stored in a retrieval system, or transmitted in any form or by any means, electronic, mechanical, photocopying, recording, or otherwise, without the prior written permission of both the author and the above publisher of this book

Paperback Edition: ISBN: 978-1533161871
This book is also available in eBook Kindle Edition

Typeset in Caslon Bold 11/14
Cover and Interior Design: Creative Gateway

Acknowledgement

With grateful thanks to my husband, Angus and my sons, Adam and Luke, for their patience and encouragement while this book was being written and for the support and help of my friends, especially Clare and Sue.

My thanks also go to Roy Baldwin at Creative Gateway for helping me to get this book into print.

Chapter One

Everyone was settled and happily tucking into their lasagne and salad when Amy glanced up to see a young man hurriedly dashing towards their table. He was tall, even taller than her for a change, with a thick mass of dark unruly curls, an aquiline nose, and deep blue eyes. Amy caught her breath. He was gorgeous.

"That's the new journalist I was telling you about who's come along to follow our group and see what an Alpha Course is all about," Kate whispered to Amy.

"Hi, I'm Craig, Craig Wilson from the Courier. I hope I have the right group. I think you're expecting me. So sorry to be late, staff meeting with the editor, I'm afraid." He smiled ruefully and held out his hand. Bill, the Alpha Course leader shook it warmly.

"Delighted to have you with us. Yes, this is your group, Craig. I'm Bill, the course leader of the group. I'll introduce you to all our members and then you must get your meal. We can't let you starve now can we?" He laughed nervously at his statement but no one else did.

Craig was introduced to the group shaking each hand in turn. Amy got up, blushing wildly when it was her turn. She put out her hand quickly and found it grasped warmly by his.

"Hi, beautiful," he said gazing at her slim body appreciatively.

Amy felt her face grow hot with both pleasure and embarrassment as she found herself gazing into his deep blue eyes, which crinkled at the edges as he smiled into her large brown ones. The moment ended with Craig striding over to the self-service counter to grab himself a dinner.

Although Craig was thin it was as if he had hollow legs and even two generous helpings of the first course, followed by apple crumble and custard didn't seem to keep him from helping himself liberally to the chocolates Bill had provided. He also knocked back his glass of wine fairly readily and seemed disappointed at just one glass being allocated to each guest but church expenses couldn't stretch to more.

Amy, for her part, felt self-conscious and couldn't enjoy her food as much as usual, even refusing the chocolates on several occasions. Each time she looked at Craig she caught him smiling back at her and winking. She soon decided not to look at him at all unless absolutely necessary.

Just before the start of the talk, which was to be given by the vicar of St James, Rev Brian Appleby, Bill considered it his duty to explain to the young journalist and others in the group what exactly an Alpha Course entailed.

"You probably know something about the layout of the evening," he began, "but perhaps I should explain further. The nine-week course begins each

Thursday with a meal and social time. There is no charge for the meal but attendees are welcome to give a donation if they wish." Amy noticed Craig smile. He clearly liked the idea of a free meal anyway. "Then Brian will give a talk which will be accompanied by film clips, music and other media. There are nine subjects in total; tonight's talk is largely an introductory talk. What is Christianity all about? Week two centres on the person of Jesus and the cross and why he died for us. Then we tackle the Bible, God's word and guidance, before our weekend away in the middle of the course—I'll give you more details about that later but the time away will deal with the topic of the Holy Spirit. Following the weekend, we will cover the questions of evil, prayer, healing and last but not least, the church."

Amy felt Bill's list was quite long and complicated to someone who had no church background. It was her mother's gentle persuasion that had led her to church when she had broken up with her boyfriend, Jake. Such a long list as Bill had just given, she mused, would have probably taken her in the opposite direction. She smiled sympathetically at Jan who didn't appear to look overwhelmed but smiled back brightly. Amy breathed an inward sigh of relief.

Brian, by contrast, kept his introductory talk very simple, making everyone laugh as he showed a short film clip about how not to talk about your faith.

Brian and his wife, Carol had arrived at St James church, Charlesworth, five years ago. Many claimed Brian had breathed new life into the church. Before then the church had been very traditional and attended only by one or two families and a few old folk who enjoyed the stability. Brian had put a few noses out of joint especially when he had insisted on removing all the pews in favour of modern padded seats.

Amy found herself sneaking a look across at her work colleague, Jan, anxious to see how she was receiving Brian's talk. Jan, personal assistant to one of the senior partners at the legal firm where Amy worked, had recently gone through a very acrimonious divorce from her partner, George, and had found things tough. Amy hardly believed that Jan would accept the invitation for the nine-week Alpha Course but Jan seemed to be listening intently, to Amy's great relief. She had been nervous about asking Jan, especially as she, herself had little knowledge of an Alpha Course. This was her first time too.

She looked across at the journalist who was also listening and scribbling copious notes in a form of shorthand script. His absorption gave her a chance to study him closer without being observed. She loved the dark, rather unruly curls and the slightly uneven nose. Her thoughts began to stray in spite of herself as she began to consider him as a man. What was he like? Did he have a girlfriend? Was he popular, a good lover? She had even got to the point of imagining herself in his arms and being kissed by him when Brian finished talking and Craig turned round and met her gaze. She blushed profusely, almost imagining he could read her thoughts, and was rewarded by another bright smile and a broad wink.

She felt mortified. What must he think of her gawping at him like some stupid, infatuated teenager? She blamed the church for that. Since coming to the small market town of Charlesworth with her friend, Kate three years ago, she hadn't met anyone remotely interesting. The twenties and thirties group was great fun socially as was the choir they were both in, but there was a distinct lack of interesting marriageable men in the church. Rob, a local computer salesman and one of the only men that answered that description had been quickly snapped up by her friend Kate. He wasn't really her type anyway, far too sensible. Mind you, he was probably exactly the sort of man she should fall for rather than Jake, the smooth talking, good looking guy who had stolen her heart a few years before. This Craig person, she realised, was quite reminiscent of Jake in many ways; too good-looking for his own good. Disgusted with herself, she got up quickly and made her way over to the coffee machine at the back of the church. Operating it she had to turn her back on the group, including him.

Discussions had begun already on her return. Amy was just in time to hear Bill suggest it would be a good idea to go around the group with each person in turn giving a short talk about themselves and perhaps, if they wished, detailing some of their reasons for being there.

Bill had long embarrassed Amy with his overbearing advances towards her. As a short, rather plump man with glasses, more towards the end of the thirties than the twenties, Amy had no interest in him. He was kind but not really her type, and she would rather remain single than consider Bill as anything more than a friend.

Bill began his explanation. "I work as an assistant in the local library," he said, "and I'm an active member of the church here in Charlesworth, singing in the choir and helping Jenny to run the twenties and thirties social group." He indicated towards a petite figure to his right with short, bobbed brown hair. "I'm here now to lead this group and I hope to answer some of your questions." He smiled and waited for Jenny to follow him.

Amy was very fond of Jenny, a woman in her forties, who although only about ten years younger than Amy's own mother, was a quiet, gentle figure readily inspiring confidence in those she was in charge of. She ran the local florist shop.

Next to Jenny was Kate and beside her the faithful Rob. Rob worked for a local computer company and was doing really well. He had already been promoted once since Kate began going out with him just over a year ago and his prospects were very good. He wore glasses and had thick sandy hair with a mind of its own. A stalwart supporter of the twenties and thirties group, he looked decidedly ill at ease with the Alpha Group but was determined to stick it out to aid Kate in her role as chief prayer support.

When Jan's turn came she was full of admiration for Amy. "Amy invited me to come on this Alpha Course," she said, smiling at her indulgently. "She's a lovely girl to work with, always cheerful about her job and rarely complaining, even though some of the solicitors in our firm take her a little for granted. I guess when she told me she was a Christian I wondered if that was her secret and I wanted to find out more."

Amy felt embarrassed by Jan's eulogy on her behalf and even more embarrassed by feeling Craig's eyes fixed upon her and was quick to explain away Jan's words.

"You're too kind, Jan," she said, her face colouring. "I simply try to get on with everyone as best as I can, there's no magic formula to it," she said and laughed lightly. "I think it's really Jan's encouragement that keeps me going." She smiled at Jan who smiled back.

Craig had a very easy and friendly manner as he introduced himself. Amy imagined that as a journalist he was used to doing this. After explaining his role as a recent recruit to the Courier with several previous years' experience on a small suburban London weekly, he went on to explain his role at the Alpha Course that evening.

"I suppose you might say I'm here to check you all out." He gave a broad, warm smile at this point, which made Amy's heart quicken in spite of herself, and continued. "But although I understand that Alpha Courses have been fairly well publicised over the last few years, many people with little or no church background don't understand the concept. I hope I can help to clarify that."

After Craig's introduction, it was left to the remaining three members of the group to make themselves known. There was the choir master aptly named Fred Sharpe, a small, fat balding man who had wild, wispy, white collar-length hair, as unkempt and eccentric as himself. He taught music at the local senior school with passion and dedication in addition to leading the choir at St James. His wife, Mavis, came with him to church sometimes but preferred her own company for the most part. Amy had a sneaking sympathy for her; she was sure if she were Mr. Sharpe's wife she might also prefer to keep her own company.

Then last, but by no means least, was Lisa the other receptionist at the Courier along with Kate. She had been to a few of the twenties and thirties socials before but not to any of the more 'churchy' events.

As Amy looked around the group, she couldn't help but wonder how they would gel together over the coming weeks and what the group members would make of Christianity. And what about Craig? What message would he give to the paper week by week as he filed his reports? He might be here in his reporter and observer role but would the message impact him personally?

Kate was surprised that Amy didn't want to stay for drinks at the end of the evening, especially when Brian, the Minister, had made it clear that he would stand the round at the local pub. Instead, she had ushered her and Jan out quickly even though Kate thought Jan would have been happy to stay a little longer. It was as if Amy was in a hurry to get away. Kate also noticed Craig watching them as they left and imagined she caught a look of disappointment in his expression. Was Amy really as averse to his charms as she was making out?

As they got back to the flat, a short drive from the church, Kate was quick to find out what Amy had thought of Craig Wilson.

"Oh ... he was okay," Amy began, in as casual a tone as she could manage, but was frustrated with herself when a tell-tale flush started to creep over her cheeks. "But rather flirty and self-satisfied if you ask me."

"But didn't you think he was gorgeous?" Kate continued. "I mean I love Rob and wouldn't think of looking elsewhere but ...," she said hesitating. "If I were unattached he could turn my head with that easy flirtatious manner of his and those cute dark curls."

"How could you even think of that?" Amy asked in irritated surprise. "He's like Jake in so many ways and what's more he's not a Christian. How could I be expected to consider him?"

Then it was Kate's turn to look embarrassed. "Of course, you're right. Probably better not to speculate."

Chapter Two

Amy was determined to put Craig Wilson right out of her thoughts during the following week but didn't find it as easy as she had hoped. His face seemed to keep popping into her mind during quiet moments at work, as well as last thing at night before she went to sleep, and even began haunting her dreams with erotic images, leaving her to imagine the smell of his musky aftershave on waking. She was sure that he hadn't even given her a second thought.

However, both girls read his report of their first meeting avidly when it came out the following Wednesday.

They certainly know how to feed you at these Alpha events. Splendid lasagne, great apple crumble too, all washed down with a glass of wine. To top it all we were even offered chocolates. Interesting bunch of people too from a slightly eccentric music teacher (aren't they all), to a stunning blonde, more likely to grace the catwalks than the church.

"I think he's talking about you," Kate commented, laughing.

"What a cheek! He refers to me as some sort of sex object rather than a person."

"Well, maybe a little. But at least he's complimentary and your anonymity has been kept."

"Yes, but it gives the wrong impression of Alpha. It's the message that's important, not the people."

Kate laughed again. "I think God would disagree with you there, Amy. Surely it's all about the people."

Amy blushed. "You know what I mean. A comment on the message is the most important thing."

"Look, it follows here," Kate said, pointing to the following section with her finger:

As to the message, well, I must say I was surprisingly reassured. Christianity was talked about but in a modern 21st century way with the use of film clips, people's stories and a few Bible quotes. We even had a few laughs at the terrible way some Christians talk about their faith. Haven't we all experienced this? At least here was no long, dull, biblical monologue, thank goodness. Next week's talk is all about Jesus himself. An interesting historical figure I think we could all say. However, church remains for many of us, a little far removed from our everyday lives and experiences and church people rather quaint. At least I have to report that this church has chairs and not old-fashioned pews.

"I suppose it's a fairly positive response, on the whole, even allowing for the bit about the church being old-fashioned, and referring to us all as 'quaint'. Although having said that, I'm not sure if that means you too," Kate said. "I wonder if Brian and Carol have seen it?"

A phone call answered the question. They had also been positively reassured for the most part.

"Might even make a Christian of him yet," Brian said jovially.

On the Wednesday before the next meeting, Kate came home from work brandishing a couple of free tickets for the races at the local racecourse the following Wednesday evening.

"They're from Craig," she explained. "He's friendly with one of the sport's reporters who gave him some free tickets for the event and he thought of us."

"Why us?" Amy asked pointedly.

"I think he likes you, that's why. I'm sure I've only been asked along as an extra, he must have seen I was with Rob. Anyway, he gave them to me at work saying that he'll see us at Alpha tonight."

She tried not to think of Craig coming again or the invitation as she dressed for the meal that night, but her heart seemed to be beating a little faster in spite of her resolve to be calm. Even Jan remarked on her appearing slightly flustered when she was picked up.

"He's a very handsome young man," Jan remarked knowingly. "If I was just a few years younger you might have some serious competition." She chuckled softly.

Amy simply smiled. What could she say?

Craig was in good time that week and was off to fetch Jan and Amy their glasses of wine almost before they'd asked.

As he handed Amy her glass he leaned towards her whispering, "Do you think you can make it to the races next Wednesday then, you and Kate?"

"Yes, I think so," Amy said softly. "Thank you for thinking of us. I've never been up to the racecourse before and to be honest I've always wanted to go."

"Good, I'm glad. I'm sure you'll love the occasion. Most folks do."

Amy realised that not all Christians thought well of gambling but she'd never found anything in the Bible to challenge the odd flutter. It was the same as alcohol she reasoned to herself, everything in moderation. She would only spend a few pounds. It seemed churlish to go to the racecourse without having just one or two small bets but it was more the thrill of the horses racing and the atmosphere that interested her most.

She didn't manage to speak to Craig the rest of that evening. Bill sat down beside him with his meal and monopolized the journalist until the talk and then led the conversation after this. Amy noticed that Craig was very interested in the concept of the cross and the idea of someone being prepared to die for him.

"It's curious," he began when the discussion got under way, "but why would someone want to die for me anyway? I mean this chap Jesus, well, he's never met me has he, never met any of us come to that. It just doesn't make sense." He cleared his throat in a slightly self-conscious way. "I mean to say, what would you say to the doubters and questioners amongst our readers on this subject?"

Amy noticed the sudden shift from personal interest to objective slant. She felt it was almost like he'd betrayed a slight chink in his armour and then quickly readjusted it, reverting to his usual role as journalist and observer. She decided she'd like to see a little more of the personal side and a bit less of the professional. She could almost imagine dying for him, never mind Jesus.

The girls stayed on at the pub for a quick drink afterwards. The pub was situated in the road just behind the church and it didn't take long to get there. The drinks were on Bill that evening and he got Amy her favourite Cinzano and lemonade without her even asking. Craig ordered a pint and joined their circle. Amy immediately steered the conversation back to the cross. She really did want to know how Craig felt about it for himself.

"Why don't you think someone would be willing to die for you then?" she asked so directly that Kate looked visibly surprised.

Craig turned his attention to her and smiled broadly but it seemed as if the serious moment of earlier had already passed. "I once had a teddy I called 'bear' whom I believed might have died for me in his better moments but that was a few years ago. I doubt anyone would want to now. After all, it's a little messy and inconvenient isn't it?" He chuckled softly.

"Perhaps you don't let anyone close enough to you to care that much," Amy suggested.

There was an embarrassed silence and a little foot shuffling before Bill came over and joined the group, asking Craig about his work as a journalist and if he was enjoying the course. The moment passed. But Amy couldn't help thinking that she detected a look of pain and sadness momentarily crossing Craig's face before the mask went up again when Bill changed the subject. She was curious. What was it about his past? Had he been hurt, even betrayed by someone close to him? Didn't he let people close to him now? Would she ever find out? She prayed as a quick arrow prayer.

God, help him to open up to you. Please make his turning to you my only desire for his company. I don't want it to become personal. Help me Lord.

Amy could hardly concentrate at work that Wednesday. It seemed unbelievable that Craig had invited her and Kate to the races with him that evening. What should she wear? She wanted to look nice but she didn't want it to look like she had made too much effort for the evening. The decision wasn't made any easier by reading the next serving of his column in the Courier. His personality seemed to come across in his writing and she could almost hear him delivering the piece to her alone.

This week's talk on Jesus and the Cross raised some interesting issues. How do we feel in the twenty-first century about the idea of someone dying for us like this guy Jesus? Surely most of us could hardly expect a close friend or partner to die for us much less this person Jesus who we've never met. The idea seems incredible and such a death rather grotesque to the modern sensibility.

She finally decided on the smart casual look. Her best and newest pair of jeans teamed up neatly with a long sleeved tee-shirt and jacket. She stood back and appraised herself in the mirror. Maybe she should have worn a skirt or a dress but would they be warm enough? The days were certainly warm for September but it was the autumn after all and you couldn't really expect a hot evening.

"Will you stop preening yourself and come on, it's time to go," Kate said in exasperation, regarding Amy looking at herself from every angle in the mirror. "We're meeting Craig at the racecourse in just under half an hour and we have to drive across town yet."

"But do you think I look okay? I mean should I have worn a skirt or perhaps different trousers or something?"

"You look lovely. Your trouble is you're the only one who apparently never seems to see it."

Craig was waiting for them outside the main entrance to the racecourse but the two girls hadn't bargained on seeing him there with a couple of other girls as well.

"Hope you don't mind Susan and Vicky joining us? They're guests of Colin the sports reporter, a friend of mine whom we owe all these freebies to."

Amy immediately felt underdressed. One girl, a blonde like her called Susan, was wearing a tight pencil skirt with a faux fur coat over it. Her colleague, Vicky, was dressed in a similar style of skirt but which was part of a smart dog check suit. Their eyes appraised Amy and Kate with almost an air of disdain. Amy suddenly felt very self-conscious like some naughty, disobedient child. Why did Craig have to invite them for goodness sake? And then she reminded herself that she and Kate were here only as guests of Craig with free tickets; it was hardly their place to complain. The girls it seemed, on introduction, were journalists and fellow colleagues of Colin and Craig at the Courier.

After handing them the little labels, which acted as passes to the racecourse, and had to be attached to their clothes, they all made their way into the grounds with Craig striding out in front with his group of girls. Kate, seeming to guess how Amy might be feeling, then took the opportunity to whisper to her, "Don't worry, perhaps the girls will go and join Colin and we can have Craig to ourselves very soon."

The racecourse was fronted by a large imposing building which on entering they found was dotted about with various food stalls, a large screen with the racing results and a number of small tote booths. Turning to Amy, Craig suggested that the two girls had a bit of a flutter.

"We don't really know how to place a bet and we certainly can't afford to part with lots of money with little chance of a return," Amy said.

"Come over with me and I'll show you how the system works."

Amy found herself grabbed by the arm and steered over to the tote by Craig. She glanced back to see that Susan and Vicky appeared rather put out by the gesture but she mentally shrugged her shoulders. Kate and she were also Craig's guests. Why shouldn't he give them a bit of his time and attention?

Craig explained the rules to her very carefully. The minimum bet was five pounds for both ways and it was better to ask for a place as well as a win which meant that you could be quids in if your horse came in the first three.

"Now, you just have to select your horse," he said, still keeping hold of her arm and pointing with his other hand to the race programme. "If you don't want to bet too much, why don't you just stick to the penultimate race? 'Royal Prince' is the favourite in that one, a local horse and at five to one, a fairly safe bet."

Amy hadn't realised that Kate and the other two girls had come up behind them as she glanced through the list of entries which meant very little to her. Quickly spotting a name which reminded her of how she felt about Craig and the two reporters, she pointed to 'Spoiling for a Win', a thirty-three to one outsider.

"That's a bit of an outsider you know," said Craig. "Not much chance of winning or even being placed. Are you really sure?" Behind her Amy could hear the amused tittering of the two girls and that decided it.

"Yes, absolutely," she said with determination.

Her seven pounds successfully placed on 'Spoiling for a Win', she and Kate then walked away from the group who were busy placing their bets on the favourite to win, 'Royal Prince', among a few other races fancied. She hardly dared to watch the penultimate race now, which she was sure, would make her out to look like a complete idiot. At least being one of the last races, she could forget about it for a while.

Craig then took them up to the press room at the racecourse. They couldn't go in but Craig entered and came out with the Courier's sports reporter, Colin, who after being introduced to them all, made his excuses to head back to his workstation, with the first race being reported as imminent.

After his departure, Craig turned to them all. "Well then ladies, shall we take our places in the stands?"

Susan and Vicky were quick to grab one of his arms apiece and march off with him towards the stands with Kate and Amy taking up the rear. As they strode ahead, Kate and Amy, although not hearing all that was said, could ascertain that the tone of their conversation was very light-hearted and flirty.

Things didn't improve throughout the evening with Susan and Vicky continuing to monopolise Craig's conversation and attention. Kate and Amy were left to their own devices, although after several races he seemed to suddenly remember them and suggested everyone join him in the bar for a drink. They all headed back into the main enclosure and Craig handed Amy her usual tipple which he'd seen Bill order for her a week earlier. Amy thanked him but felt slightly irritated that he hadn't thought to ask what she would like to drink. She would have much preferred a soft drink as it happened, not wanting to show herself up in any way in front of the two young journalists. But she realised she was probably being churlish. It was nice of him to remember such a small detail and one Cinzano and lemonade was hardly going to make her drunk.

Things, however, didn't improve with the girls. Kate and Amy felt completely ignored while the flirting and giggling went on with Craig. He was obviously a favourite in the office since his arrival, Amy thought bitterly.

At last, it was time for the penultimate race and the party took their places once again in the stands. But the results were not at all as expected. The favourite refused a jump halfway round the course and a few other well-known jockeys and horses fell and then there was her little mare, a chestnut filly, galloping up in third place as the winning post came into view.

"Oh come on 'Spoiling for a Win'," she shouted enthusiastically, as inwardly she thought it would be good to win and prove to those two confident flirts that she wasn't such an airhead as they might think. Sure enough, the horse did her proud, coming in at third and she was seventy-seven pounds better off for the experience.

"Beginner's luck or maybe you've found the thing you are good at," Susan said in a slightly sneering tone

"Perhaps I have," Amy answered sweetly, but her victory seemed slightly hollow as Craig was still being monopolised by Vicky and Susan and only stopped briefly to congratulate her. Finally, he asked her if she wanted him to help her collect her winnings from the tote.

"No, I think I'm quite capable of simply showing them my winning ticket and collecting the cash," she said coldly.

He looked surprised but replied, "Very well."

"I'll come with you if you like," Kate offered.

"Yes, please."

Craig then suggested that they exit the racecourse before the final race in order to avoid the crowds and seek out a pub for a drink and some food.

"Let's find somewhere within walking distance," he suggested. "We can collect our cars later when the queues have dispersed."

Amy felt despondent in spite of her win and was inclined to go straight home, queues or no queues but decided it would be rather mean-spirited of her not to offer to buy a round of drinks with her winnings. As they all strode off to the pub nearest the racecourse, again it appeared as if she and Kate took up the rear on their own as Craig and the two girls went on ahead, laughing and flirting together. When they arrived at the pub she immediately offered to buy the round of drinks.

"Are you sure?" Craig asked. "I was all set to buy the drinks for everyone."

"No, please let me," Amy replied, promptly. "After all, I understand journalists aren't that well paid and I did win a reasonable amount."

"She has a fair point," Vicky said. "We journalists are at the bottom of the pecking order of professional pay."

Amy thought she saw a look of annoyance momentarily cross Craig's face but she could have been mistaken.

The flirting and joking continued as they sat round a table together, with Vicky and Susan monopolizing Craig's attention.

"Shall we order some food now?" Craig said after a while, looking across at Amy and Kate.

"You go ahead," Amy said quickly, "but if it's alright Kate and I really must go as I have an early start at work tomorrow." Kate looked at her questioningly but Amy continued on. "Thanks for a great time. I'm obviously a natural at the racetrack."

Her voice sounded a little strained even to her own ears but she was close to tears and desperately fighting to retain her composure.

"No, please stay, we won't be that long."

Almost for the first time that evening Craig fixed his gaze on her and his tone sounded quite imploring and full of genuine regret.

"Sorry, but we simply must dash. Thanks again."

Amy knew she must hurry before she gave him the satisfaction of breaking down in tears in front of him. She and Kate marched quickly up the road and round the corner to the car park before Amy gave vent to her tears of anger and humiliation.

"It's not what you think," she said, quick to reassure her friend. "I'm not interested in him in the slightest degree; he's nothing but a shallow flirt. But how humiliating to be made to look foolish by those girls. I dare say he thinks us foolish too, a couple of silly little religious nutters. I expect he only asked us to swell the numbers. After all, it's better to be seen out with four women than just two isn't it? Does great things for the ego. I bet they're all laughing at us now. Poor little innocent Christians they'll be saying."

"Well, there's no excuse for his bad behaviour even if he is a flirt but perhaps the evening didn't turn out for Craig quite as he expected either," Kate said.

"Maybe not. But he's not a Christian and I'd sooner live and die a spinster, terrible though that sounds than be subjected to become the wife or girlfriend of someone like him. No doubt he'd be constantly cheating on you. You couldn't trust a man like that. Look at Jan's George and how he let her down."

"Yes, it does appear so," Kate said, and that was the end of the subject between them as the girls picked up a Chinese on their way home and tried to forget all about their rollercoaster of an evening. Meanwhile, Amy wondered about tomorrow night's Alpha Course. She knew that she had to go because she couldn't let Jan down but she didn't know just how she was going to be able to face seeing Craig again, that is if he even turned up.

Chapter Three

Events took a strange turn with Kate arriving home from work the following evening holding a large bunch of red roses. "They're from Craig," she said slightly bemused. "He grabbed me just as I was leaving work and presented me with these as a kind of apology to both of us for last night. He said he'd behaved shamefully and felt really bad about the way in which he'd all but ignored us, claiming that Susan and Vicky were rather domineering."

"Oh really, blame it on the girls," Amy said curtly.

"Well, he did go on to say that he was truly sorry for the way in which things had turned out, I must say," she said after a moment's consideration. "He did look rather sorry too, giving the appearance of someone who hadn't slept that well."

"I expect his two lady friends kept him up most of the night," Amy said, flinging her handbag down on the settee in an irritated fashion, the same way she'd like to have flung it at Craig.

"The roses are nice but they don't change anything for me. He's still an incorrigible flirt, playing off one woman against another. He probably just picked up the roses cheap at the local supermarket anyway."

"No, I don't think so," said Kate, peering closely at the label. "No, these are definitely best quality ones from the florist and there's even a card attached." She pulled it off and handed it to Amy while she took the flowers through to the kitchen in search of a vase.

Amy opened the small envelope and saw Craig's untidy scrawl across the card:

I'm really sorry for letting you both down and behaving so badly. Please forgive me. Love Craig xx.

Amy sniffed in disapproval. He certainly wasn't getting any kisses from her. He clearly was the type who bestowed his kisses far too casually. If he turned up at Alpha tonight she would be impervious to his charms. After all, the main purpose of Alpha was to take Jan and help her understand what Christianity was all about, wasn't it? Now what should she wear this evening?

"I'm going upstairs to change," she yelled out to Kate. "You can read his grovelling little note if you wish. I've left it on the table in the lounge."

She was still deciding what to wear when Kate yelled back up at her. "Two kisses eh, I wonder what we can read into that? Anyway, I must be going, got to get to the prayer meeting before the meal. I'll see you and Jan there?"

"Yeah, see you later, "Amy called back. She had tried to convince herself that she didn't care about Craig at all and wasn't interested in his opinion of her or her clothes but she still managed to try on three different combinations before settling on a pink flowery skirt with a pretty hemline. After carefully applying her makeup, she then remembered that her current handbag, which she had thrown down on the settee earlier, was black and consequently had to dig out her new pink one and transfer all its contents before she was finally ready. It was then she discovered to her horror that time had marched on and she was late in leaving the house to collect Jan.

She hastily gave her a phone call and managed to reach her just in time before Jan went out the door.

"I'll pick you up in ten minutes," she breathed hurriedly, "I'm afraid I'm running late."

"No problem my dear. Did they keep you at the office again?" Jan asked sympathetically.

"Err ... yeah, something like that," Amy muttered quickly. She wasn't about to explain her unsettled state of mind. She didn't even want to admit it to herself.

When Amy and Jan dashed into the church hall everyone else was busy eating. After a quick hello to all, they went straight up to the self-service table to collect their meals. Amy noticed Craig was deep in conversation with Bill when she arrived and hardly gave her more than a cursory glance.

Well, she didn't care anyway. He certainly didn't give the appearance of someone deeply ashamed of his behaviour on the previous evening.

However, after the evening had finished without Amy and Craig exchanging more than a brief hello, he suddenly grabbed Amy's arm when Bill suggested drinks at the pub nearby.

"Please say you'll come, Amy," he began. His tone was imploring. "I need to buy you a drink to make up in some part for last night, although I know it won't go far in doing so."

Bill, overhearing something about last night, was all ears, saying, "Last night? What happened then?"

"Just a trip to the racecourse," Amy answered casually.

"The racecourse eh? Hardly a suitable place for a young Christian lady like yourself."

Amy glanced across at Craig and to her annoyance he was smiling. It probably made him think that Christians didn't get out enough.

Not knowing what to reply to Bill's remark on the spur of the moment, Amy continued her conversation with Craig. "I think Jan wants to go home early tonight and so does Kate," she said, "so being the chauffeur, that's not going to be possible."

"Why don't I borrow your car?" Kate suggested. "I do have to get back and if Jan is also keen to get home I'm happy to take her if that's okay with you? Maybe Craig could give you a lift home?"

"Delighted."

Damn Kate. What was her game?

Amy gave her friend an angry look but it appeared lost on Kate. She was also annoyed with herself realising that she was looking forward to the pub visit and being driven home by Craig afterwards much more than she should. In the end, it was only Bill, Craig and her who went on to the pub that evening and with Bill dominating the conversation with talk about the Bible and reading, Amy kept quiet.

She was interested to learn, as she'd expected, that Craig was an avid reader especially of biographies, which was perhaps understandable given his interest in people's lives. Deep in thought, trying to sum him up from his choices, Amy found herself being addressed by Craig in a somewhat persistent tone.

"Is that true Amy, is that what you read?"

"What?"

"You were miles away. Bill says you like to read romances and chick lit. Is that right?"

Amy blushed. How foolish she must seem to him.

"Well I do, but I read other stuff as well," she insisted, looking angrily at Bill who appeared not to notice. "I regularly read one of the weekend broadsheets especially the arts section and my writing magazine ..."

She tailed off quickly. She hadn't meant to give away so much about herself but perhaps Craig wouldn't notice.

He was, however, quicker on the uptake. "Writing magazine? Are you a writer then, Amy?"

Amy felt suddenly shy and embarrassed. "Well, I've always had dreams of becoming a writer but ... silly isn't it? I mean even if I was any good it wasn't really an option open to me. With my Father dying when I was just eight and my Mother struggling to keep both me and her, it was a case of going and getting a job as soon as possible."

"That's a great shame," Craig said. "But surely you could still do some writing after work?"

Amy sighed. "I'm often too tired when I eventually get home and to be honest, without having any real encouragement, I suppose I lost the inclination."

"Didn't your mother encourage you?"

"She tried to, yes, but ..."

Amy hesitated. It made her mother seem unkind which she was far from being. "She was too busy trying to keep things together; she didn't really have the time."

"Let's not talk of writing all night," Bill said impatiently, feeling rather left out of the conversation.

"I just think it's a shame and that the world is a poorer place for not being exposed to Amy's talents," Craig continued, on a topic close to his heart.

"You flatter me too much, I'm sure," Amy said, blushing. "I gained good marks for my stories at school, that's all. After that, it was a case of getting off to secretarial college and learning a career."

"Well, perhaps one day you'll get another chance," Craig said.

"I can't see that happening anytime soon. Dreams don't pay the rent."

"No, they don't," Craig replied thoughtfully. "I had dreams too, which is why I do what I do. Perhaps I could help you. We obviously have quite a lot in common."

Bill, who was now feeling even more left out of the conversation, began to insist. "Amy and I have quite a lot in common too. We belong to the same church and hold similar beliefs."

Craig held up his hands and smiled somewhat mockingly.

"Point taken. I never suggested otherwise. Ready to go now, Amy? I have to make an early start in the morning."

"Yes, that's fine." She was also tired having not slept that well the night before.

Amy was surprised as Craig led the way to a rather impressive racing blue Jaguar sports car. It looked expensive, and as she got in she surveyed the interior complete with leather steering wheel and suede covered seats, and felt suddenly cold and sick at heart. Even if it wasn't brand new, Craig and his colleagues had given the impression that journalists were badly paid. Something didn't add up. Perhaps Craig had some other secret source of income. She suddenly shivered involuntarily.

Craig glanced across at her with a concerned look on his face. "Cold?"

She shook her head vigorously.

"I can give you my jacket if you want?"

Amy, impressed by his manners gave another vigorous shake of the head.

"Oh well, if you're sure."

There was a momentary silence and then Craig spoke as he started up the engine and they moved off. "Look, I still feel bad about last night. It was only meant to be a little bit of fun, I never intended for anyone to get hurt."

"You flatter yourself thinking you hold such sway," Amy said in an irritated tone. "Kate and I are good friends and happen to enjoy each other's company anyway. And we did have to leave early. What you and your colleagues get or got up to is none of my business."

Craig looked rather sheepish. "Nothing happened," he said, "nothing at all. We just had a quick meal and were home within an hour."

They drove the rest of the way in silence and soon reached Amy's door. She undid her seat belt and moved to get out but Craig detained her by a gentle hand on her arm.

"I know I may seem shallow," he began. "But I do have feelings, really I do."

Before Amy knew what was happening, he had reached across and pulled her into his arms. His gentle kiss on her lips quickly developed into much more as he gently pushed her lips apart with his and she felt the pressure increase as his tongue made contact with hers and she spun dizzily into an embrace where she was rapidly losing control. His breath also seemed to become shallow as his arms tightened around her, crushing her into his chest so that she could barely breathe.

After a few minutes, he released her. They were both breathing quickly and for a moment gazed at one another in surprise.

"Well, thanks for the lift, I guess I'll see you next week," Amy said quickly, feeling embarrassed.

He nodded and then said in a quiet voice hardly more than a whisper, "Bye."

She stumbled from the car in a daze, finding her keys and letting herself in, hardly daring to look back at the car, although she knew he was still there watching her. Perhaps he was seeing that she got in safely. That was chivalrous.

Thankfully Kate was already in bed asleep so there was no need to explain anything. As Amy went up to bed she knew that she wouldn't get much rest that night either, she had too much to think about: *What am I going to do Lord? This is becoming too personal. I'm just fooling myself that all I want is for him to believe in you. Well, I do want that more than I can say but I'm beginning to want him for himself too, much more than I can admit. Help me fight this attraction God, I know it's wrong but it's too strong for me to fight on my own. Help me, please.*

She kept going over and over the events of the evening. Craig's interest in her writing and her opinions, and most of all, that kiss. That had really unsettled her.

In the early hours of the morning, she finally fell into a deep, restless sleep filled with images of Craig.

Chapter Four

Amy spent the first half of the week floating on air, reliving the kiss again in her mind but for the rest of the time castigated herself for having entertained such impossible dreams. But the truth was the kiss had felt good and she was sure it had surprised him almost as much as her. He'd said that he did have feelings. Did that mean those feelings were directed towards her? The thought made her heart beat quicker and brought a flush to her cheeks.

Next morning Kate had asked, "Did everything work out okay with you and Craig last night?"

"I don't know what you mean," Amy said quickly. "He only gave me a lift home, that's all, nothing more. He can only ever be a friend. He's not a Christian and doesn't seem very close to making any sort of commitment, does he?"

"Well that's hard to say," Kate said. "It's true that he doesn't share our faith at the moment and it would be difficult to get involved with someone who couldn't share such a large part of your life."

"For goodness sake, Kate, I'm not about to get involved with him."

"No, I know. But it's a shame. In so many ways you are both perfectly suited."

"Please don't let's fall out over this," Amy said curtly. "You thought Jake and I were suited, don't you remember?"

Kate blushed. "Of course, you're right. He probably wouldn't be faithful. It's not right for you to get involved. Sorry."

"Apology accepted. Let's not talk of this again."

Kate felt sad for her friend. She knew Amy's faith was her life and that marriage to someone who didn't or couldn't share it was out of the question for her, but it was a shame Craig wasn't a Christian and was such an incorrigible flirt.

Amy felt guilty. She'd told her friend that she had no intention of getting involved with Craig, but hadn't she done that by letting him kiss her? It was hardly a quick friendly peck on the cheek. Such a kiss had demanded a response and one she had been only too willing to give. She blushed at the recollection of her eager response.

What would he be thinking now? She was looking forward to and dreading the next Alpha meal in equal measures. His latest written thoughts on the bible didn't help to calm her beating heart either:

Many of us keep a copy of the bible on our shelves, but how many of us have actually read it? Probably not that many, it might surprise you as it did me. However, how many of our common sayings originate from there, such as 'a nagging wife is like a dripping tap'? Great stuff in my opinion.

Amy's cheeks flushed with sudden anger. Why on earth was she letting such a man invade her thoughts? His column showed him out to be a male chauvinist with little respect for women in view of the saying he had chosen to highlight. What about some of the others which were much more positive like 'a good wife is more valuable than jewels?' That was in the bible too.

She read the end of his column.

Apparently, it seems the bible is still the world's bestselling book which is amazing in this day and age. Maybe it is worth another look?

On the following Thursday, Bill began to encourage them all to sign up for the Alpha weekend. He seemed to take it for granted that Amy would be going and Jan was also very keen to go, especially after hearing that the weekend was to be set in Blaen Bae Conference Centre in the middle of the Welsh countryside. Bill explained that the centre, as the name denoted, was close to the Welsh coastline and equipped with sports facilities and a heated indoor pool. Of course, he was quick to say they were expected to share rooms with the cheap rate they were getting.

"I have no problem sharing with Amy," Jan said, "if she's willing." Amy nodded at this point. "Especially with all the rooms having en-suite facilities. The place sounds great. I don't think the weekend stay feels like a hardship, far from it."

"Of course, we don't expect you to join us," Bill said to Craig. "We've appreciated the publicity that your column has given to Alpha but we really don't expect you to come away on the weekend too, which

I'm sure is well outside your paper's requirements of you."

"No, really, I'd like to come. The place does sound great and I feel I could hardly write a column about an Alpha Course and then leave out one of the key parts—the weekend. Besides, it doesn't sound like much of a hardship to me either, staying in a conference centre with a heated swimming pool, even if we do have to share rooms."

At this point, he looked across at Amy who blushed furiously at the thought of sharing a room with Craig.

Bill noticed the look exchanged between the two of them and in a tone of irritation, quickly added, "Of course it's couples of the same sex only that will be sharing, with the exception of married couples. We can't be giving the place the wrong impression of a church group, now can we?"

He finished by giving both Craig and Amy a fairly severe look but Craig simply responded with a smile alongside a light-hearted, "Well, you can't blame me for trying can you?"

Bill cleared his throat in a continuing tone of annoyance. "Before we all go away on the weekend together it is a good idea to get to know one another a little better." He looked over at Amy with a slightly wistful look at this point. "So I suggest a social this next week. It's getting rather late and cold for a barbeque in October, but we could all have a 'bring and share' meal or alternatively perhaps a session at the local ten pin bowling alley?"

The latter was the preferred option and so the following Tuesday was proposed and accepted with nearly everyone being able to make the date except the Sharpes.

Amy wasn't great at ten pin bowling and she feared making a fool of herself in front of Craig. She was sure he would be good at it. He struck her as the sort of person who would be good at anything he put his mind to.

The two alleys were booked for 7.30pm and they had all changed into their bowling shoes and begun the first game when Craig came breezing in. Another late night meeting with the editor he explained.

The group occupied two alleys and with the other alley being full, Craig was slotted in at the end of their group. It was Amy's turn next and she tried hard to concentrate on getting a strike but was only too aware of Craig's eyes watching her every move. Consequently, she threw the ball a little weakly down the alleyway and was mortified to see it skew over to the gully at the edge and disappear out of view without a single hit.

"Never mind, you may get a hit on your next go, Amy," Bill said jovially.

But the next go didn't produce a much better result with Amy only managing to hit two of the ten skittles in both of her attempts. Craig would think her very silly. She sat down despondently not looking at Craig, only to find he had sat down beside her in the seat that Bill had just vacated for his turn.

"Your ball could be too heavy for you and you're probably not swinging it fast enough or with the right precision," he said. "I could easily show you a better technique on your next go if you'd like me to."

"Oh and I suppose you're an expert," Amy said, slightly caustically.

This appeared to throw Craig a little off guard. "No, I'm not expert, not at all. It's just that someone showed me a good technique for play and I thought I could share it with you, but if you don't want me to, don't worry I …" He trailed off unsure of what to say next.

Amy suddenly felt mean. He had only been trying to help her for goodness sake. What was she so jumpy about?

"I'm sorry, I must have sounded very ungrateful. Forgive me. I just get so fed up with making a fool of myself."

"Well, that certainly could never happen to you," said Craig now smiling and looking a lot more at ease. It was his turn now to show if his technique could work. Yes, it was good. A strike in one.

"Well," Jan said, leaning over to whisper quietly to Amy before Craig returned to his seat. "Very impressive in more ways than one."

Amy knew she was referring to more than just his bowling skills.

"And something tells me that he's not unimpressed with you either, my dear."

Amy blushed but couldn't think of anything clever or witty to say in response. And then it was her turn again. Craig jumped up with her and before she knew what was happening had grabbed a burgundy coloured ball on her behalf and had his arms placed around her trying to position her arms and body for the strike. Well, that's what she told herself anyway, but she loved the feel of his arms around her and could cheerfully stay in that position without worrying about throwing the ball at all. But Craig helped her to bend properly and guided her throw which also turned out to be a strike in one. Everyone in the group cheered on her return to her seat except Bill that is who looked somewhat annoyed. The evening ended by Craig being the all-out winner, followed, to her great surprise by Amy and then Bill. Bill seemed disgruntled at being upstaged by Craig and Amy when he was used to being the all-out winner at the twenties and thirties socials, but he still managed to shake Craig's hand graciously and plant a quick peck on Amy's cheek along with a gentle hand squeeze.

Amy glanced across at Craig and noticed a look of sudden annoyance cross his brow, but it was gone in a moment as he reached past Bill to press a warm and more persistent peck on Amy's other cheek.

"Well," Kate began, once they had dropped Jan off and were alone together in the car. "How does it feel to be fought over?"

"I don't know what you mean," Amy said, trying to sound ignorant.

"Oh I think you do," Kate said knowingly. "How funny that Craig should even be just a little jealous of Bill. I think I know who you'd prefer if you could have him." And she chuckled quietly.

Amy was annoyed at herself that the tell-tale blush once again seemed to find her out, and she couldn't think of anything to say. To lie would be to look even more foolish and she hardly dared own up to the truth. What was she going to do about her growing attraction to this man? It was wrong, but she was feeling more and more out of control of her own feelings and didn't like to even guess at his.

Chapter Five

The following Thursday was spent in making the final preparations for the weekend. Amy's car was rather small and she was nervous of the long drive down the motorway and only too relieved when Bill offered to drive her, Jenny and Jan in his car. Bill owned an old Ford Mondeo saloon, steady and sedate just like him. Amy found herself mentally comparing it to Craig's sleek sports car and smiled to herself as she considered how much the vehicles suited their driver's characters. Kate was, of course, travelling down with Rob and her work colleague Lisa, and the Sharpes had offered to take Craig in their estate car.

"No, but thanks for the offer all the same," he had said. "I often have to work late on a Friday night and consequently don't think I'll be able to make the five o'clock set off that most of you are anticipating. It's probably better if I make my way alone. I'd hate anyone to have to rely on me. I only have room for one extra in my two-seater sports car, anyway."

As he finished the last comment a somewhat wistful look was sent in Amy's direction and slightly embarrassed she looked away quickly. In fact, she was rather glad not to have to travel alone down the motorway with Craig for close on two hours. She knew the church wouldn't approve of two single people being thrown together for quite so long anyway but hardly dared to imagine how she would keep her cool in such circumstances. And what about him? Would it compromise his driving to spend so long in close proximity to her?

She immediately chided herself. She was presuming he had a strong attraction to her which was foolish. She was willing to bet that Craig Wilson probably had a strong attraction to any female under the age of thirty, he certainly gave that impression.

That night's topic, 'God's guidance' made Amy feel uncomfortable as she heard Bill, in his usual glib and cocksure manner which seemed to leave little room for doubt or debate, state. "God has a perfect plan for each of our lives. He gives us all certain gifts and abilities which he then uses to direct our choice of career."

"I wish I had your faith, "Amy began, "some of us didn't have a choice in our career. Rather that choice was dictated to us by circumstances and financial considerations."

She tailed off suddenly realising that her anger had got the best of her and she felt ashamed as she saw Bill's expression. His jaw had dropped open with surprise and she realised what a poor witness she must sound to an unbeliever.

"It is hard for Amy," Jan began by way of explanation. "I know she finds life at Brookes and Bradbury rather difficult. She is often taken for granted by some of the partners, especially the more senior ones."

"I'm sorry," Amy said, "I didn't mean to take out my personal grievances on others."

"I think it's a disgrace that someone young and willing to please like Amy should be used like that. She's far too good to be a servant to some fat and comfortable group of lawyers," Craig said, warming to his subject.

Everyone looked at Craig in surprise.

"I didn't realise that you were quite so unhappy, Amy," Bill said. "Perhaps we could close in prayer for you."

Amy felt embarrassed by her sudden outburst now and more than a little puzzled by Craig's vehement defence. She needed to defuse the situation and fast.

"Umm, yes I would value your prayers but I'm sorry. I don't know quite what came over me. My job really isn't that bad. After all, if I didn't work at Brookes and Bradbury I wouldn't have got to meet Jan. I think Craig's probably being a little kind in my defence. I'm not sure what else I could be doing if I wasn't there. God did guide me to that job in Charlesworth which is a place I love. I have made some very good friends here and I know I'm very lucky to have a job."

It was a long speech for Amy, who was usually quiet. Once she had finished, she immediately fell into a silent contemplation of her feet saying nothing else for the rest of the evening. She beat a hasty retreat at the first available moment when the meeting ended, declining a trip to the pub.

"Craig must think a great deal of you to defend you so vehemently," Kate said when the two girls were finally alone in the car.

"I don't know about that," Amy said, blushing. "I only wish I had kept my big mouth shut now. I feel ashamed at my outburst. I'm hardly a great witness for my faith."

"I don't agree," Kate said. "I think in some ways if people are going to believe, then they'll be far more attracted to a faith where you can be open and honest and air your grievances and hurt, rather than a faith where everything is always happy-clappy all the time. People will respect your honesty. Craig certainly seemed to."

Amy read Craig's write-up about guidance in the paper later that week:

Guidance is a sticky area for all of us, with or without faith. We can often wonder if we're on the right course for our lives, whether we consult our horoscopes, mediums or God. You might think that Christians have got it all right. A perfect line to God implies being in the perfect career or calling. Not necessarily. It seems that Christians are often at the mercy of their circumstances like all of us, as I learnt only this last week. God may be with them but He's not the sugar daddy who hands it all to you on a plate. Perhaps God is a realist after all?

A realist, she thought. Hmm ... that was an interesting twist on God. She wondered what he meant by it.

Amy was ready and waiting when Bill drew up in his car at 4.50pm. Jenny was already in the front of the car with Bill and offered to sit in the back but Amy immediately rejected the offer, insisting that it was better she sat in the back to keep Jan company. She was relieved to have the excuse of avoiding two hours of Bill glancing her way continuously and being drawn into frequent conversation with him.

Following Amy's directions, Bill drove slowly and steadily to Jan's home. Bill's driving was like his character, steady and entirely predictable. What would Craig be like set loose on the motorway? She was sure he would at least up the pace on Bill.

Because Bill was such a steady driver, the four of them arrived only just in time for the meal at 7.30pm.

Even in the growing dusk, Amy could see that the Blaen Bae Conference Centre was large and imposing as they made their way up the drive. She imagined the place had made a good family home at some time in the past. Fortunately, it had adequate parking on either side of the house and even in the gathering gloom, they could all see the grounds were fairly extensive and promised a few good walks, benefiting from the location's proximity to the Welsh coast.

As the evening was moving on, they only had enough time to collect their name tags and itineraries and dash upstairs to their rooms, depositing their luggage just inside the door before making their way to the dining room, where everyone was now seated. Amy glanced around quickly as they made their entrance but saw no sign of Craig.

"I think he said he was coming on later," Jan said smiling and knowing exactly who Amy was looking for. "Isn't that Bill waving to us to join his table at the back?"

"Yes, it is. Is that okay with you?"

"Of course."

They had finished their meal, unpacked, had their first introductory meeting from the manager of the conference centre and were busy organising their evening schedule when Craig sauntered in and joined them, giving Amy a quick wink. Amy noticed it was just after nine o'clock.

Many of the Alpha guests had opted for a visit to the local pub, which in view of the dry, cold evening boasted a short bracing walk of around half a mile.

"I must say I rather fancy the walk and drink at the local myself," Amy said, slightly uncertain, but was disappointed when all of her group seemed to favour watching the latest James Bond film on video instead. It was quite good but she had already seen it once at the cinema with the twenties and thirties group and had no desire to see it again.

The rest of the group only became aware of Craig's presence when he said, "Well, I'm up for that, I'll join Amy if she wants."

The thought of leaving Amy to Craig's clutches made Bill hesitate. "Well, I've seen the James Bond film already, I suppose I could go to the pub too."

Amy didn't want Bill to come. She realised that she would like an opportunity to get to know Craig better and perhaps talk to him more about her faith which would never happen with Bill around, so she quickly countered. "I know you don't like pubs that much Bill and that you'd prefer the film. It's okay. I'm sure Craig will look after me and there are lots of other people going too."

As Bill looked around at the large group assembling for the brisk march to the pub, he seemed to reconsider. "Yes, of course, that's true. Safety in numbers they always say, don't they?"

Amy glanced across at Craig and saw him raise his eyebrows at the implication. She couldn't help smiling. He was a lot less safe than Bill but that was part of the attraction.

The group for the film slowly dispersed upstairs, as the pub group began to make their way outside for the walk. Craig didn't appear to be quick to join them.

The room was nearly empty when Amy said anxiously, "Shouldn't we be joining them or we won't know the way?"

Craig smiled. "I didn't want to say anything with the others around but would you mind a slight change of plan?"

Amy looked disappointed. Maybe the film wouldn't be so bad a second time around if Craig was beside her.

Catching her drift, he quickly added, "No, not the film. I'd rather spend time with you than James Bond. But what would you say to a drive out a few miles from here to find a pub all to ourselves?"

This was definitely much more dangerous and exciting and Amy knew that it wouldn't be approved of by either Bill or the church. But what the heck? It was a golden opportunity to get to know him better without anyone else around.

Amy smiled. "Okay, but will I be safe with you?" she quipped, smiling.

"Oh no, I shouldn't think so," he replied, laughing.

"Then I immediately accept," she said, hoping that he took her response in the joking way it was meant.

Craig was quite the gentleman as he opened the door of his sports car for her and settled her inside. The walkers had left by now and they had the car park entirely to themselves as Craig jumped into the driver's seat and started up the engine.

"I suppose you did get a meal when you arrived?" Amy asked suddenly.

"Oh yes, there was a plate of fish and chips awaiting my arrival and very welcome it was too."

"When did you get to the centre then?"

"Just around 8.30 which wasn't too bad as I'd only left just before seven."

Amy laughed. "That was a lot quicker than Bill. We left Charlesworth around five pm and didn't get the guest house until 7.30pm, just when everyone else was going in for dinner."

"Steady, reliable old Bill," Craig remarked sardonically.

"He is very kind and thoughtful too," Amy said defensively. She felt comfortable enough to have a little joke at Bill's expense herself but didn't like to hear him openly mocked by others. After all, he had been a good friend to her when she had really needed one.

"Yes, I'm sure he is. No offence meant," Craig said quickly.

They drove in relative silence for most of the journey with Amy wondering if she had been wise to accept Craig's invitation. She hardly knew the man.

Then, rounding a corner, they came upon a thatched cottage pub with a large wooden sign outside announcing that it was the Thatcher's Arms.

"Poor man. I wonder what happened to the rest of him," Craig said facetiously. "Let's stop here, it seems like a nice place."

Amy nodded positively and soon they were inside the warm and cosy pub, boasting a huge log fire in the corner. "Just what you need for a night like tonight," Craig said. "What can I get you to drink, your usual tipple?"

"Yes, please, I'll go and find us a seat over by the fire, shall I?"

"Yeah, that'll be good."

Amy found a small table just to the right of the large fire and sat down, pulling off her large coat and scarf and draping them over the back of the wooden chair, as she stopped to look around her. The place was fairly full but one got the impression it was mainly populated by locals from the unanimous nods of recognition accompanied by greetings generally exchanged in a strong Welsh dialect. Glancing towards the bar, she saw Craig gently push his way forward in a calm, confident manner as he waited to be served. He was soon strolling towards her with her glass and a pint of bitter for himself.

"Nice place," he commented. "Strong local flavour."

"Yes."

"What do you want to talk about then?"

"You. I feel I hardly know you."

"What do you want to know?"

"Everything."

"Hmm ... dangerous."

Amy noticed a look of uncertainty even slight fear cross his face, but it was gone in an instant as he slowly began to open up.

"My father was a senior judge before he retired just under ten years ago. Of course, he thought his only son should succeed him in the profession and was horrified when I elected to choose journalism instead. I'm a great disappointment to him. A 'mere scribbler' in his eyes."

The last lines were spat out with a hint of bitterness in their tone, and in spite of herself, Amy couldn't help reaching across and covering Craig's hand with her own. "Oh, I'm sure he must have changed his mind by now when he sees how successful you've become at what you do."

Craig gave her hand a quick squeeze. "You're very kind but not everyone is as kind or sweet as you, my dear Amy."

Amy blushed at the endearment and encouraged Craig to continue. Now she understood better why he had been quite so vehement in her defence about her being the so-called 'girl Friday' at a law firm. The very nature of the business must rankle with him.

"Not that I spent a lot of time with my parents during my childhood," he continued. "They've always been wealthy and Annabel and I seemed to get in the way of their grand lifestyle."

Money ... hmm, Amy pondered. That perhaps explained the presence of the expensive Jag on just a small journalist's salary.

"As soon as I could be sent away from home I was. I must have been about seven or eight when I was packed off to a preparatory school in London whilst my parents continued to live out their busy and hectic social life in the south of England."

Amy looked horrified. "Weren't you lonely or was Annabel with you?"

"No. She was sent to the equivalent girls' school. And yes, I was lonely. I remember crying myself to sleep every night for the first few weeks."

"Oh Craig, I'm so sorry," Amy said, putting an arm around his shoulder.

Craig gave a quick dismissive smile. "It's okay. I don't cry myself to sleep too often these days."

Amy realised the statement might indicate years of loneliness and insecurity but felt it best to keep quiet in the meantime. After all, Craig had just begun to open up to her and she didn't want to risk losing any trust which she might have won through overstepping the mark.

Craig went on to explain how he had excelled in English, even winning a national story competition while he was still at school but this all meant very little to his father who believed that boys should only excel in the sciences and maths and that the arts were just for girls.

"Didn't your mother stand up for you then?" Amy said, sipping the drink she had largely forgotten about until this point.

"No. Mother simply followed Father in everything he did and accepted his opinions, even though he'd cheated on her for years and she knew it."

Amy was horrified. How could people live a lie like that? But then she thought about Craig's behaviour at the races and his flirtatious nature and wondered if perhaps he wasn't just a chip off the old block too.

Verbalising her feelings, she said, "That's terrible. I wouldn't be able to keep silent if someone cheated on me."

Craig nodded, "Yes, it is sad."

However, his lack of judgement on the matter of infidelity made Amy wonder if he didn't secretly approve of such behaviour, even if not in his mother's case.

Finishing her drink and glancing at her watch, she said, "Don't you think we should be making a move? It's quite late and if we're both missing at some late hour it might arouse suspicion." She stood up and pulled on her coat and scarf.

"Yes, you're right, we should be going." Craig drained the remainder of his mug and also stood up and pulled on his coat. "But I haven't heard your story yet."

"I'll tell you about my life in the car if you like but there's not a lot to tell."

"I don't believe that and it's a deal."

As soon as they were settled in the car Amy began.

"My Father died when I was very young and my mother struggled to bring me up on her salary working in a local dress shop. Things improved a little when I started secondary school and mum became the manager of the shop but money was still tight. Also, when she worked longer hours I missed her being around as much, but at least I was able to go to Kate's home for a couple of hours or so after school each day. That's why we're so close, we practically grew up together. I had writing aspirations from an early age and taught myself to word process so that I would be able to enter competitions, but when Kate went to secretarial college it was more practical to follow her. I had to put my desires on hold as earning a salary was a more important concern. I owed it to Mum who'd had to keep me all those years."

"Yes, I've been very lucky to have the luxury of being able to choose my own career, even if it was one which didn't win my parents' approval."

As Craig said those last words, Amy saw him glance quickly in his mirror before pulling across the road into an adjacent lay-by. As he turned off the engine, Amy looked around her nervously, glancing towards the door for a way of escape. Had she really been such a fool to come out alone with a man she hardly knew and to trust him not to try and seduce her?

Craig noticing her nervousness immediately said, "Relax. I'm not going to take advantage of you or anything like that. I only wanted to give you a goodnight kiss if that's alright with you. We may have already aroused suspicions at the conference centre if anyone's noticed us missing together, but kissing in the car park there would create an even worse impression. So can I kiss you, Amy?"

Amy realised he was right and relaxed. A kiss from him was more than alright, in fact, she had been thinking about it for most of the evening. "Yes, that's fine," she said in a small and slightly nervous voice.

Craig leant across the car and took her gently in his arms. Like the last time, his kiss was gentle at first and then as she responded almost against her better judgement, became more passionate. After a few minutes, true to his word, he released her. Amy noticed that his breathing had quickened along with her own and that the car seemed to have steamed up but not a word was said between them after the kiss until they reached the grounds of the centre.

As he turned the engine off, he turned to her and leant over to give her a quick peck on the cheek before saying, "You'd better hurry inside quickly before anyone sees us. Thank you for a lovely evening, I've really enjoyed it. I'll see you in the morning."

Amy stepped out of the car pulling the door shut behind her and with a quick wave ran towards the large double fronted doors at the rear of the guest house. Remembering the number code, which the manager had told them all for late comers, and glad that she'd had enough presence of mind to scribble it down on a piece of paper for Craig, she rushed inside and up to the first floor room she shared with Jan. Opening the door quietly and hearing slow, regular breathing, she realised that Jan was already asleep, which was perhaps just as well. Otherwise how on earth would she explain the late hour?

Amy found sleep eluding her. She tossed and turned for what seemed like hours, hearing nothing in the stillness but Jan's regular breathing and the steady tick-tock of Jan's alarm clock. She smiled as she considered that she hardly needed an instrument like that to wake her when she hadn't as yet got to sleep. She could still feel the touch of Craig's kiss on her lips. As she thought through some of his revelations about himself she felt a real empathy with him. He'd had a tough childhood. He just needed to find real love. Then she immediately chided herself. What was she thinking of? The fact remained he was still a womaniser and a flirt and not for the likes of her. He wasn't a Christian like her and she had no guarantee that the Alpha Course would make him one. It was all about free choice wasn't it, which meant he also had the choice not to receive Christ. What then? How could she share her life with a man who could never understand the most important thing in the world to her, her faith? She prayed alone in the dark:

God, please help me, events are moving out of my control. I shouldn't have let him kiss me I know, but I wanted him to so much. What is wrong with me? Please help me I don't know what to do.

Chapter Six

She had worked herself up into quite a fever with restlessness and had to get up twice in the night for a drink and the toilet. Finally, as it grew light, she got up quietly, showered and tied up her still wet hair, dressed and sneaked out of the door onto the landing. Some of the staff had started work and so the main door was already unlocked. Amy slipped outside enjoying the bright, crisp morning, silently praising God for it when she realised she wasn't alone. A solitary figure was seated on the wall in front of her also contemplating the beauty and as she got closer she knew it was Craig and her heart did a little flip. He, sensing the approach of someone, turned around.

"Couldn't sleep either, then?" he asked smiling.

"No. I've even had time for a shower and it's still a while until breakfast. Was Bill a noisy roommate?"

"I should say so. Snores loud enough to wake the dead. Mind you, I'm not sure I could have slept that well even if he had dozed like a baby. You gave me a lot to think about."

Amy coloured at being the subject of his thoughts.

"And you me," she said so quietly that Craig could only just catch the meaning.

"Seems silly to walk alone now you're here. Want to join me?" and he put his hand out inviting her to hold it. As she took it she felt the pressure of his fingers closing around hers, so warm and reassuring. They walked in silence for a few minutes each lost in their own thoughts until Amy decided she should explain a little about the format of the day.

"This is perhaps a good time to explain to you just what to expect today," she began carefully. "We start after breakfast with a short talk about who the Holy Spirit is, you've probably seen that on your programme, but nothing too heavy. He's just God living inside of us if you like." She coloured as she thought this might sound rather silly to the uninitiated. "Then, after coffee, we continue on with what the Holy Spirit does."

"I sure hope it's nothing weird. I don't know whether I could cope with that." Amy noticed his guard going up again as he said, "After all, some would say I'm quite weird enough already," and he laughed a little uncertainly.

"Oh no," Amy said quickly. "Bill says this is just a talk about what the Spirit has already done in the Bible. It's after our free afternoon that we get to see what he can do for us, and don't worry, the Holy Spirit is a gentleman and would never make you do anything you didn't want to do."

"On that note, as a gentleman I hope I can escort you into breakfast?" Craig asked, giving her a mock bow. "I'm sure I just heard the bell."

"Yes, I heard it too. Delighted, Sir," she responded with an answering mock curtsey and a little gleeful laugh. But she was sad that the bell had intervened as an excuse to end their discussion about the Holy Spirit. As they drew near to the door, Amy took her hand out of Craig's with a little shake of her head. Understanding her meaning for discretion he didn't try to take hold of it again, and they went into breakfast with a crowd of others so as not to arouse suspicion.

Looking around the dining room as people settled at the various tables, Amy spotted Jan nearby. "There's Jan over there. I feel I owe it to her to sit with her. We haven't spoken since yesterday evening. She must wonder where I've been."

Craig nodded in agreement. "And Bill's also next to her," he said. "I probably owe him some explanation too."

"Hi Jan, Bill," Amy said, as they approached.

"I was wondering where you'd got to," Jan said. "You must have been up really early as you'd gone before I even woke, and you weren't in your bed when I went to sleep last night but you've obviously been busy," she continued, smiling and looking from Amy to Craig.

Bill intervened. "Yes. I've been wondering where you've been too, Craig. Now I know."

"You know exactly where we've been," Amy intervened, her irritation being directed at Bill rather than Jan. "We went to the pub last night and this morning I was up early walking in the grounds when I came across Craig doing the same thing. Surely that's not a crime?"

"No, of course not," Bill mumbled. Not sure where to take the conversation next, he fell silent as the cooked breakfasts began to arrive.

Over breakfast Bill explained the programme for the day in much the same way as Amy had, although with slightly more jargon. Amy found that she was really hungry after her restless night and early morning stroll, and managed to tuck away three small slices of toast as well as the cooked breakfast.

"All that walking must have made you hungry," Jan said who had struggled to finish the breakfast and only one slice of toast."

"I like a woman with a good appetite," Craig added, tucking into his fourth slice of toast and marmalade.

"Well yours is even better than Amy's," Jan said, smiling and pushing her chair away from the table. "Do you mind if I go up to our room, Amy, I've one or two things to sort out before our first session?"

"No, of course not. I'll come with you if you like."

"No, no hurry, you don't have to. Stay a bit longer if you want."

"Well, I can't sit jabbering all day," Bill said on a note of some irritation. "I've got things to organise. You coming, Amy?"

"Umm ... no. If you don't mind I'll just sit here for a little while longer, someone needs to keep Craig company while he finishes his breakfast. I usually have to rush mine most days. It's a pleasure to have the time to just sit and chat."

Bill looked from Amy to Craig with more annoyance. "I suppose it depends on the company," he said, getting up and leaving the table with an angry strut.

Craig chuckled. "Someone is a little jealous of me I think."

They were now the only two left at the table so Amy felt able to speak her mind.

"Jealous, I can't think why. I've never given him any reason to think of me as more than a friend and perhaps you flatter yourself that you are also the object of my attention," Amy said, feeling suddenly hot.

"Oh, I hope not," said Craig flashing her one of his most disarming smiles. "I had begun to feel that we had something special between us."

Amy felt out of her depth. The fact was she was a Christian and Craig wasn't and a flirt to boot. Focusing on the last thought she said with a spark of exasperation, "I suppose you say that to all the girls."

"No, only the pretty ones," Craig replied facetiously, but seeing the look of disappointment cross her face that Amy was struggling to hide, he quickly changed tack. Grasping her hand under the table he whispered, "Amy, you do realise I was joking just now, don't you, and that I'm serious?"

The smile had left his face to be replaced by his blue eyes gazing into hers with a look of utter sincerity, and dare she believe it, love?

Smiling and looking down with some embarrassment all she could think of to say was, "I don't think this is the time or the place, Craig. Shall we go?"

"Yes, of course."

Leaving the dining room, they went their separate ways without any further conversation except a quick, "See you in the meeting then," from Amy.

She was one of the last in the first session, the turmoil in her feelings making her slow to get ready. She was disappointed to see that Craig was already there with Bill sitting beside him. Even Jan had found a space beside Kate and Rob, but looking around quickly she spotted a space right behind Craig and headed straight for it.

They opened the meeting with a couple of songs which had become familiar to the whole group since they had started singing songs at the Alpha meetings in the last three weeks. Amy had never stood near enough to Craig before to hear him sing but was pleased to hear his resonant tenor voice was both tuneful and pleasant compared with Bill's deep tuneless bass. For someone who enjoyed music and singing as much as she did, this was important.

Then Brian came to the front and with the aid of hastily drawn 'stick men' which accompanied the Alpha material, began to explain the role of the Holy Spirit in the scriptures. Craig was immediately drawn in and it looked as if he was taking in each and every word. Even at coffee time she wasn't able to talk to him, but instead found him deep in conversation with the young worship leader from the church called John, a person she hardly knew. The second talk explained some of the miracles and gifts of the Holy Spirit, and again she could see Craig listening quietly and attentively.

Jan and Amy went back to their room before lunch to put their Bibles and notebooks on their beds and freshen up. By the time they returned to the dining room, most people were already seated including Craig who was sitting next to Brian the vicar and seemed to be deep in conversation with him. Then they saw Bill waving at them madly from a table in the centre of the room, there were just two spaces left on either side of him. Amy suspected that he had saved the places for Jan and herself.

Over a lunch of cold meats, cheese, coleslaw and jacket potatoes, they discussed their plans for their free afternoon. Bill and Jan were in favour of a trip out to the seaside nearby, around half an hour's drive from the conference centre and Kate and Rob, also on their table agreed. Amy wasn't sure. She felt in need of space to gather her thoughts and feelings and was also keen to try out the small indoor pool at the Centre.

"Actually, would you mind very much if I stayed here instead?" she asked, watching Bill's enthusiasm for the plan fall away. "There's been a lot to take in and I feel I need some space. To be honest I wouldn't mind trying out the pool here either, not to mention catching up on a little sleep."

"So you won't change your mind no matter who comes with us?" Bill said, glancing deliberately at Craig's table to his right.

"No," Amy said with determination. Why should she care what Craig did with his afternoon? She was set on hers whatever.

"I'll ask Craig to join us then at the seaside if that's alright with you?" Bill persisted.

"Why should that matter to me," Amy said crossly. "I've already told you, my plans are set."

Nevertheless, there was still a part of her that felt she could almost be tempted to change her mind if Craig were going out with the others. No, even if he did, she argued to herself, there would be no privacy to talk privately or to find out any more about him. Far better to stay and try to work out her own churning emotions.

Amy decided she would go down and see the party off, persuading herself it was the right thing to do. She felt guilty that she had left Jan to her own devices for much of the weekend so far, although Jan had assured her on more than one occasion that she really didn't mind. But she had to admit that she was also a little curious to see whether Craig was joining the others or not. Even the Sharpes were going and taking Jenny with them. But Craig wasn't with the group as Bill soon confirmed.

"That seems to be all," he said in a peremptory tone. "Kate and Rob are taking me, Jan and Lisa in one car and Fred and Mavis Sharpe are following in their car with Jenny. Amy and Craig have both elected to stay here."

Kate, Jan and even Lisa threw a few knowing smiles in Amy's direction. She was glad he was staying here, but she was sure that it was his own decision entirely and nothing to do with her. He probably knew nothing of her plans. Perhaps he was staying on to continue his conversation with Brian, she mightn't even see him. Secretly she hoped she might.

After waving them off and wishing them all a good time, Amy went back upstairs to try and catch up on some sleep before her swim.

However, after some time tossing and turning again on the bed and another short time of praying for wisdom and guidance for the relationship and the way forward, she decided that enough time had lapsed between lunch and her rest to make a swim reasonable.

Making her way downstairs to the pool and exchanging her clothes for her new blue costume, she was surprised to find she was almost alone except for two young girls from the worship band. After saying a brief hello to them she relaxed and looked forward to a good stint of exercise and relaxation to get rid of some of her tension. She had only swum a couple of lengths before the girls got out and she found herself completely alone with only the lifeguard for company, a young lad who looked rather bored and fed up as if he wished he were elsewhere. Well, that was tough. She needed a swim and the pool wasn't due to close for another hour yet. Halfway through her fourth length, as she approached the deep end of the pool once more, she spotted Craig.

He was lined up at the deep end and ready to make what she suspected would be a rather spectacular dive. As she gazed up at his tall body, lined up and ready, she found it hard to concentrate. His trunks were well fitting and his lean chest muscly and well formed. In her confusion, her concentration lapsed momentarily and she slipped beneath the surface, choking from the water she had taken in. Gasping a little, she made her way up to the deep end and grasped the chrome bar at the end.

His attention was drawn at once to her choking form and he leant down towards her, a note of concern in his voice, "Amy, are you alright?"

Amy glanced across at the young man who had also dismounted from his perch debating as to whether or not he should come across. Amy shook her head at him.

"I'm fine," she spluttered a little embarrassed. "Just a bit surprised to see you here that's all."

"Yeah, I decided to stay and try and catch up on some sleep, generally take things easy. I didn't really fancy an afternoon out at the beach today."

"Me neither. Get any sleep?"

"No, not really."

"Me neither." They both laughed.

"Look, I distracted you," she said. "Sorry. Don't let me put you off your stroke. I'll stay here at the side and you can go ahead and do your dive."

He did and was soon in the water alongside her. "Fancy a piggy back?" he offered.

Amy nodded and guiltily climbed onto his back as he swum effortlessly back down to the shallow end of the pool. After a few such rides and a few more lengths, Amy felt cold and decided it was time to get out.

"Do you mind if I get out now, I'm getting cold," she said, shivering.

"Of course not. I'll just swim a few more lengths and probably see you later?"

"Yes, will do. The next session's at five pm, after tea and biscuits in the lounge."

"See you there then. Nice costume," he added admiringly as she climbed out of the pool.

"Thanks, it's new. See you later."

After showering, drying her hair and reading her Bible for a short time, Amy made her way down to the lounge. She was ready for the biscuits and tea after all that swimming and she looked out expectantly for Craig but he was nowhere to be seen. Well, perhaps he had managed to have that sleep after all. She'd probably see him in the meeting. But he wasn't there either, a huge disappointment to Amy as she'd prayed and prayed that in this session about meeting with the person of the Holy Spirit, God might meet with him and perhaps even fill him with his Spirit.

Bill didn't seem to know where Craig was either as leaning across to Amy at the start of the meeting he whispered, "Any idea where Craig, is Amy?"

And she'd had to admit that she'd seen him at swimming but that was around an hour ago. After this, she tried to concentrate on praying for Jan and her marriage situation but felt really guilty as she struggled to concentrate her mind.

He didn't turn up to dinner either, a lovely hot shepherd's pie and veg. Amy should have been hungry after her swim but in her worry about Craig her appetite had vanished. Jan watched Amy pushing her food around the plate and said quietly in her ear,

"I'm sure he's okay. There's probably a very simple explanation for his absence like he's been called back to work."

"Yes, I'm sure you're right," Amy said in a non-committal tone which didn't betray the stirred emotions inside of her.

Then before the evening's entertainment began, Bill took his place at the front of the large room by the microphone, much to his group's surprise.

"Just before the entertainment starts," he began, "I'd like us all to pray for one of our team members, Craig Wilson. He's just phoned me on his mobile to let me know that he's heading for London to collect his sister and to fly off to France where his parents have been involved in a bad car accident. He doesn't know any of the details yet but it must be sufficiently bad for the police to contact him and his sister in the UK. Craig has only come on Alpha as a local journalist to follow the course for his paper, but let's pray that through his circumstances he might find faith for himself."

Bill followed on with a prayer but Amy didn't hear any of the words of it. All she could think of was Craig and how he would be feeling. She knew that he and his father didn't have a very good relationship and wondered how he would be taking the news of the accident. And how bad was it really? Why hadn't he phoned her? Then she remembered that they hadn't exchanged mobile phone numbers. Why hadn't they? Didn't he trust her enough to give her his number? No, that was silly. No one could have suspected something of this nature to happen quite so suddenly out of the blue. Of course, Craig would have Bill's number as the leader of the Alpha group. As the prayers finished, she felt Jan's arm around her and was grateful for the contact.

"We'll keep praying that everything will be okay and not as bad as expected eh?" Jan whispered and Amy nodded, she felt too overcome to speak.

Amy sang her karaoke song that evening to the accompaniment of the worship band. Everyone said she sounded great but her heart wasn't really in her singing. She also found it hard to raise a smile for the jokes and skits and was relieved when the entertainment finished around nine pm.

Another visit to the pub was suggested but this time, Amy's heart wasn't in it. Instead, she followed her group upstairs for the film, a thriller with a fairly complicated plot line. Amy found these films difficult to follow at the best of times, but with her mind elsewhere that evening, it was well-nigh impossible and in just under an hour she found herself getting up and making her excuses to Jan and the rest of the group. At least she could say she was tired. She was exhausted, although once again sleep seemed to elude her and she heard Jan tiptoeing in just over an hour later. Not feeling much like talking it was easier to feign sleep. But as she drifted in and out of sleep, she had reason to believe that perhaps, at last, God had answered her prayers. He knew she was weak and that her feelings for Craig were getting out of her control and he had intervened at last by removing him entirely. Maybe that was for the best. If that was so, why didn't she feel that way? And why did his

removal have to be under such painful circumstances? She prayed to herself:
It's not a great situation for him to be in, Lord, although maybe it will it help to bring him to faith? Please be with him, Lord, and comfort him. Amen.

But she couldn't be sure that even a tragedy like this would bring him to faith. No, it was better to forget about him altogether. He wasn't likely to be attending the rest of the course now and she wasn't likely to see him again, was she? Probably all for the best. But although she tried to convince herself this was the case, her heart still seemed to disagree.

The rest of the weekend passed in much of a blur to Amy. The communion service, the group sharing time and finally the Sunday roast dinner. She wasn't that inclined to talk in the car on the way home either and was irritated by Bill's speculations about the accident.

Chapter Seven

Craig had managed to write a few words in the Courier about the weekend in Wales in spite of his circumstances. It read:
Great weekend in the heart of Wales at the lovely Blaen Bae conference centre surrounded, not only by the lovely Welsh coast but also the countryside, good food, a great pool and even better company. Interesting discussions about the more personal side of God, the Holy Spirit.

Here, Craig's piece ended with a note from the Editor: *Due to unforeseen personal circumstances, Craig Wilson will be away for a few weeks. The Alpha column will now be continued by Sammie Young in his absence.*

Unforeseen circumstances? The note pierced Amy's heart. Yes, completely unforeseen circumstances indeed.

"Sammie Young? Kate said, noting the replacement. She frowned. "That doesn't bode particularly well for the column I'm afraid."

"What do you mean?" Amy asked.

"Sammie Young I'm afraid is a well-known atheist. Her views, unless something drastic happens to her, aren't going to be especially sympathetic. I'd better warn Brian and Bill."

The Alpha session following the weekend was on the question of evil and spiritual attack. It seemed entirely appropriate to Amy in the light of Craig's parents' accident and the way it had intervened to stop him meeting with God and finishing the weekend, even if it had prevented their relationship developing further. There was a part of her that felt that it didn't really seem fair of God to lay down the rule about only dating Christians, especially when the church held such an inadequate supply of Christian men and many of those were wimpy. Craig was sexy and desirable. He just wasn't a Christian. Did that really matter? No, she mustn't think like this, when she knew he was an incorrigible flirt. Her thoughts were becoming more and more wayward themselves.

In spite of the small, mousy-haired journalist, Sammie, who seemed to wear a continuous sneer on her face, Amy, was encouraged that the subject seemed to cause Jan to ask more searching questions. Amy was all too afraid that her preoccupation with Craig over the weekend might have discouraged Jan.

But the newspaper report of the subject the following week outraged them all. The articles seemed to have lost Craig's punchy delivery style and interested probing and, true to expectations, had taken on a rather sceptical tone.

The report began:
This week's topic of evil didn't answer the questions that many of us ask. World tragedies, famines and disasters were glossed over with a simple explanation of the sin in the world being due to our free choices. As if we would choose such disasters. This seemed

naive at best and at worst cruel. A few of the members did share about how God had met them in difficult circumstances, but the talk succeeded in giving no satisfying answers to the eternal questions.

Amy was livid. "Did you see how this Sammie person has dealt with Craig's column?" she said in a protective tone. "I'm sure he would have had a more positive message."

"No doubt," Kate said. "Sammie's true colours are certainly showing."

"Why then did the editor choose her as Craig's replacement?"

"Tactical, I suspect," Kate said. "I had heard they thought Craig's column was too positive. They're now presenting an alternative viewpoint. The editor doesn't have much sympathy with Christian beliefs. I was surprised he wanted to do the column in the first place to be honest, though I suspect it might have been to hang the Christians out to dry. I don't think he was very happy at the way Craig had handled the assignment. I'd heard Craig had suffered a few lectures over it."

"Well, I think he did a great job," Amy said with feeling.

"We all did," Kate replied, but noted Amy's vehement defence of him with growing alarm.

There was still no word from Craig when they learnt about prayer in week seven. Amy wished that he had been there to find out how to bring God into his situation but prayed for him in his place.

The newspaper articles remained sceptical:

Talking to God, our subject for this week. I guess that's a good one for those of us who want to talk to ourselves without embarrassment. But who can believe anyone really cares enough to listen to our small concerns.

On week eight they discussed healing. Amy prayed with real fervour for Craig's parents to be healed and for Craig and his sister to be helped in their grief by emotional healing. The newspaper column only carried the words:
Christian healing can, for the most part, be explained by the power of positive thinking as indeed can all the spiritual disciplines that would tell us otherwise. The Christians tried to convince me with their personal stories of God's intervention which, for the most part, could be explained away by happy coincidences.

On the final week, Bill, at last, had some news and produced a card for them all to sign.

"I have had another phone call from Craig," he began. "He and his sister are on their way back to the UK; actually, they might already be there as it's been a few days since he rang me. They're staying at his sister's flat in London for a week or so. I got the address from him and thought it would be nice for us as a group to sign a card and post it off to them to show that they are in our thoughts and prayers."

Everyone agreed that this was a good idea. Amy wasn't sure quite what to write when she knew the others would see her greeting and decided against the love and kisses she wanted to add to her name, settling instead, for a 'God bless, thinking of you, Amy'.

Well, the 'thinking of you' was certainly true. These days she rarely seemed to do anything else.

Then Bill added, "I'm away at a library conference on IT in the workplace tomorrow." He paused as if waiting for applause. "So I won't have enough time to post the card. Does anyone else pass a post box on their way to work?"

"I do," Amy said immediately. She lied. In fact, she would have to go out of her way to go past the main post office box which was the nearest, but she had begun to formulate a plan in her mind that had very little to do with post boxes of any kind.

"Good, well done," unsuspecting Bill said, gratefully.

In truth, Amy was desperate to see Craig again and couldn't bear the thought of him being back in this country without seeing him. It had been almost three weeks since she last saw him and that seemed a lifetime ago. After all, she reasoned, Craig was staying at his sister's flat so what harm could there possibly be in her popping in with the card and passing on her best wishes to them both from the group and herself?

She sneaked the London A-Z map into her room that night and poured through the street names at the back, trying to match up the address with the areas on the map. Luckily the flat was fairly central, near Earl's Court, so she decided she could take the train and tube with just a short walk at the end.

Next day after work, which luckily she finished early, she would make her way there. She didn't need to stay long and could ring her mother who was always pleased to see her for a bed overnight. With those thoughts in her head, she lay down in a frenzy of excitement at the thought of seeing Craig once more and prayed silently.

It's only a visit of one friend to another, honestly God. I know that he can never be mine. All I'm going to do is deliver the card personally to him and his sister and then come home. Surely that's better than just receiving the card in the post? That would be too impersonal and uncaring, wouldn't it God?

It was with these thoughts and others of a similar nature that Amy occupied her mind on the train the following evening. Was she doing the right thing? Wouldn't she appear a little eager in her visit? They were only supposed to have arrived in the UK recently and might be out. Amy began to regret her eagerness so much that when the train arrived in London she was tempted to get the very next one back.

But swallowing her fears, she got onto the underground tube to Earls Court station and with the map in hand traced out the progress of the streets until she arrived outside the large communal door with its intercom system. Taking her courage in both hands she rang the bell beside the name Annabel Wilson.

She was surprised when it was Craig's sleepy voice that answered rather than his sister's which she had expected but told herself immediately it was entirely natural he should answer his sister's doorbell.

"Craig? It's Amy. I've brought a card for you and your sister from the group. Can I come up?"

"A ... Amy?" There was a slight pause as if he was inwardly digesting the information. "I'm afraid the place is in a bit of a mess, but you'd better come up."

The sight of Craig shocked Amy. He came to the door wearing jeans and a baggy old jumper more than a few sizes too big for him. His hair looked tousled and unbrushed, and he sported a growth of stubble as if he hadn't shaved for a while.

Seeing her surprised look, he ran a hand self-consciously through his hair.

"Look, I'm sorry," Amy began. "I hope I haven't woken you or called at an inconvenient time? I can just leave the card I brought with me and make myself scarce."

She cleared her throat self-consciously.

"No, no, please come in. I ... It's really good to see you, Amy."

"Umm ... Where's your sister Annabel?" she asked, looking around the flat for evidence of her. It seemed to show obvious signs of neglect. There was at least a day's worth of dishes in the sink and empty drinks bottles and papers littered everywhere. It gave the impression of a male bachelor pad rather than a young girl's flat.

"Oh, she was going to come with me but then we decided at the last minute that mother needed her support for a little longer."

"So your mother wasn't killed in the accident then?"

"She wasn't even in it."

"What?"

Craig sighed. "There's a lot to explain, I don't even know where to begin."

"You don't have to tell me anything if you don't want to."

"But I do want to. You don't know how good it is to see you again. Come here."

Hesitantly she went forward not sure what to expect, whether he was going to kiss her or break down. They hugged each other silently and then drew apart. She could smell the strong whiff of alcohol on his breath and felt uneasy.

"I've needed to do that for a while and wanted to talk to you but I didn't have your phone number."

"No, I didn't have yours either and I daren't ask Bill for it."

Craig smiled briefly. There was an awkward silence between them as Amy opened her handbag and drew out the card.

"Here's the card," she said, passing it across to him. "The reason why I came. It's signed by all of us. I could have posted it but well ... I wanted to see you."

"Good. I'm glad you came."

"I suppose I should go really." She shuffled her feet in embarrassment. "I mean without your sister here, it's a little awkward isn't it?"

"Oh come on. Surely you and I don't need to stand on protocol. I really want you to stay and besides ..."

77

He paused with another thought seeming to occur to him. "It's already growing dark and I'm not happy about you going home on the train on your own so late."

Amy's heart soared at the note of concern and care in his voice. "I could stay with my mum. She's not too far from here."

"Oh, please stay. I really want you to stay."

His pleading tone tore at her heart. She could see that the flat needed a big tidy up and he looked like he needed a good meal at the very least as well as someone to talk to. Christians are supposed to care for those in need aren't they, to show the love of Christ? Surely she should do that for him? What harm could there be in that?

"Right," she said, taking off her coat with determination and hanging it over the back of a nearby chair. "I'll set to work on these dishes and tidying up the flat and then we could have something to eat. By the way, when did you last eat?"

"I don't know really, this morning I think." He ran his hands self-consciously through his hair again. "Yeah, probably this morning."

He didn't seem entirely sure and looked thinner than she remembered. "I'll make us a cup of tea first if you like. You do have tea bags don't you?"

"Yes, I think Annabel keeps them up on the shelf to the left of the sink."

Amy found them and put the kettle on but when she came to look in the fridge for the milk she began to gauge how grim things really were. All there was in the fridge was a small pint carton of milk and half a bottle of white wine, nothing else. She glanced across at him.

Catching her meaning he said, "Yeah ... I haven't been shopping for a few days. Meant to but ... oh, I don't know. Look, I know there are a lot of dishes, but would you mind very much if I took a shower and changed? This really isn't my best outfit."

She smiled. "Well, I have seen you wear better, I must admit." She was rewarded with an answering smile.

Apart from a few plates and a few empty microwave cartons, which she threw into the bin, most of the dishes on the worktop were bottles, an empty whisky bottle and several bottles of beer. She imagined he hadn't eaten much for a while. His meals seemed to consist mainly of the liquid variety. Eventually, as she was coming to the end of the pile, Craig emerged in a fresh pair of jeans and an open-necked shirt, clean shaven and with freshly washed hair. As he came across to her at the sink and put his arms around her she caught a whiff of his fresh, spicy after-shave. He wasn't making it easy for her to try and remain detached from her feelings.

Trying to concentrate on the job in hand and keep her feelings in check, she detached herself from him saying, "Just let me finish these dishes and then you can fill me in with the takeaways in the local area.

"There's a very good pizza place just around the corner which Annabel and I have often used," he said, grabbing a tea towel from the drawer and drying up the last few remaining dishes. "Do you want me to give them a ring while you finish up here? You've been really marvellous, thank you."

"That's okay," she said smiling, "and yes, pizza is fine with me but can we order a small side salad between us too?"

"Certainly, I would probably have done that anyway. What toppings do you like with your pizza?"

"Oh, I'm not fussy. Just order what you like and I'll be happy."

"Fine."

As the pizza place was only just around the corner from the flat, they were sitting down to the meal within half an hour. Amy had taken care to set the table nicely, filling two glasses with the remainder of the wine and warming the plates in the oven. Neither of them said much during the meal which Craig devoured as if he hadn't seen any food for several days. As they ate, she filled him in with the nature of the Alpha columns in the Courier since his departure.

"I'm not surprised," he said with a rueful expression. "The editor and I had one or two disagreements about what I'd written. He's quite a sceptic you know, and I think Sammie's an out and out atheist."

"Oh yes, she certainly is. I hope you didn't suffer too much on our behalf?"

"No, not really," he said dismissively. "Is there any coffee to finish? I'm not sure if there's any in the cupboard."

That sounded very suspiciously like he hadn't looked before, Amy thought, getting up and taking their plates across to the sink.

"Yes I've found some filter coffee," she called back.

"Is there enough milk for it too?" he asked.

"Enough for one which is fine given that I take mine black."

"That would be nice then, thanks."

As Amy carried the two mugs of coffee across, she realised that Craig had moved away from the table and was now seated on the settee. He patted a place beside him for her to sit. After a few minutes' silence, he said, "I guess it's time to fill you in with the details of the accident and ensuing events".

She didn't know what to say in response and just nodded.

He went on to explain that after arrival in France, Annabel and he had discovered that their father's car didn't contain the bodies of their parents, as expected. Instead, the two bodies were that of his father and a family friend, Rosemary Evans. Both had died at the scene of the accident. "So you see he remained unfaithful right to the end." Craig spat out this last piece of information with a real sense of loathing, the suffering etched out on his features. This intensified as he struggled with telling her of the tears of his sister and his mother, who grieved deeply for her unfaithful husband, even though he had never been faithful to her beyond the first couple of years of marriage.

"It must have been unbearably difficult for you having to stifle your own feelings in order to comfort your mother and sister," she said with careful feeling. "After all, he was your father, even if he was a bit of a cad." She hesitated. "You must have still loved him?"

"Yes in a way I suppose I did. Even though I continued to disappoint him right to the end," he replied bitterly. "It makes me sick when I think of him, The Judge, deciding other people's morals when his own life was such a huge lie from start to finish. Evidently he didn't care about being honest to my mother or to me and Annabel. He was always so sanctimonious, pulling me up at the slightest thing when he ..." He shuddered and Amy put her arms around him expecting him to break down and the tears to come, but instead he grabbed her roughly and began kissing her with intensity.

She practically cried out with the violence of his emotions but knew somehow that this was his way of coping, pouring out his agony and heartache into her. Well, she loved him, she knew that now and she was happy to absorb his suffering and make it her own if that's what he needed. But Amy was surprised at how quickly things seemed to progress, from that first comforting, slightly rough kiss to the slow parting of her blouse and bra as he began to run his fingers over her bare nipples. This shouldn't be happening, she knew all that with her rational mind but it was so delicious, so arousing. Her blouse and bra discarded he began to undo her trouser fastenings.

"No Craig, we shouldn't, mustn't ..."

"Shouldn't, mustn't what?" he said in between kisses. "Who says we mustn't?" As if to prove the question irrelevant to him, he began pulling off his own clothes too with an increasing sense of urgency.

"Stop," Amy called out, "we mustn't, I mustn't. We have to stop."

The desperation in her voice suddenly alerted him and he stopped his hasty undressing.

"What is it, Amy, darling?"

His voice was both tender and soothing and could lull her into a sense of the rightness of the situation, stop her from fighting with her own desires, but reason managed to maintain its fragile hold over her. She knew she had to stop him, stop the situation from developing any further. She was embarrassed by her own state of undress before Craig and increasingly aware that she was seeing more and more of his bronzed, well-formed body.

"I'm saying that we mustn't go any further, I mustn't," she said and with an almost supernatural effort she pushed him away from her and began to retrieve her clothes now lying in a heap on the floor. She heard him laugh a mirthless laugh.

"What the hell are you doing?" he said abruptly. "I thought …"

"Well you thought wrong," she said caustically. "I'm not that kind of girl."

"You could have fooled me. I thought you were well up for it," he said, almost forcing the words out of him.

"How dare you!"

"What I mean is ..." His tone became gentler and more controlled.

"I was mistaken, you are mistaken," she said. "I shouldn't have stayed. I have to leave. I'm still a virgin and as a Christian, I intend to stay that way until I marry. Until ..." She hesitated now feeling used by him, just another of his conquests. "Until I find the man I love."

She didn't want to add that she'd already found him, didn't want to make herself look even more ridiculous in his eyes than she must already look at that moment. Oh God, dear God, how had she let herself be such a fool? Persuading herself to stay in the flat with him alone as some gesture of Christian magnanimity? She must be truly naïve. She now realised how different it must have looked to him. As if she had stayed in the flat alone with him for one reason only and now she was denying him the very thing he expected.

"A virgin eh?" he said, slightly bemused. "Well ... I can be gentle you know. I won't hurt too much."

"You don't get it do you?" she said angrily. "I'm not going any further with you, I shouldn't even have gone this far."

He suddenly seemed to realise she was serious and let out his breath in a slow exasperated sigh. "You're right there," he said angrily. "You led me on and now just expect me to go away and be a good boy. I'd better get out of here before I say something worse."

He got up and walked angrily towards the bathroom grabbing a pair of pyjamas from the chair as he went. His tense form and the way he moved betrayed his anger. He was livid because of her.

As soon as he left Amy burst into tears, chiding herself for her stupidity and regretting making him angry. She couldn't stay. She would have to leave, late though it was. She began dressing hurriedly sobbing all the time and was about to retrieve her coat when he returned.

"Where do you think you're going?" his tone was softer now and betrayed a note of concern.

"Home or to my mother's. It's probably better if I do."

"No way. I wasn't happy about you leaving on your own earlier on in the evening and I'm certainly not happy now it's after midnight. No, you'll have my sister's bed and I'll take the single bed in the guest room."

"I've only brought my makeup and a toothbrush. I didn't really expect to stay."

"Wait here. I'll get you one of my shirts to wear as a nightie."

He was back in a moment and almost threw the shirt in her direction. "Goodnight then."

"Goodnight."

He really hated her, he hadn't even tried to comfort or talk to her. She knew in that moment their relationship was over if it had ever had a chance in the first place—and that was always doubtful with her being a Christian and him not. He for one seemed to have drawn a very definite line under it, under her.

Amy spent the night tossing and turning and crying into her pillow until she felt completely wrung out. As soon as the light began to filter through the curtains she rose, washed and dressed quickly. Her face betrayed her tired and restless spirit as she gazed in the mirror at the dark circles under her eyes and her pallid, blotchy complexion. Her first thought was to buy some breakfast for him as there was nothing in the flat. But how would she do that without a key? She daren't wake him to ask. And then she saw it. A set of keys with both a Chubb and Yale lock on them. It looked right. She tried the Yale in the front door just to check. Yes, it fitted. She had to assume that the Chubb would fit the large external door too.

The sleepy city was just beginning to crawl into life as she got outside. She wandered past the pizza take-away which was now most definitely closed and prayed that being London and just six am she would be able to find something open. She soon found a small Greek delicatessen tucked around the corner of a neighbouring street. It would do nicely. Here she could purchase some yoghurts, a couple of pints of milk and a pack of croissants.

"You're up early, my dear," a large, plump Greek man said, who she took to be the proprietor.

"Yes."

Amy smiled a faint smile. She wasn't in the mood for conversation even though she knew the man was only being friendly and after paying him she quickly left the shop.

On her return, she could still hear Craig sleeping deeply. But she was relieved to hear he didn't snore.

She began to chide her silly thoughts. What did it matter anyway? She was never going to see him asleep any time in the future. A silent tear dropped on to her cheek and she brushed it away angrily. She had to be strong now, walk away whilst at least some of her dignity remained.

She made herself a black coffee and ate a small pot of yoghurt. She couldn't face anything else. She would leave the rest for Craig. Then at least he'd have something to eat that day. Then she thought, she must leave him a note but what would she say? Pausing a moment and sucking the end of her pen as she considered, she finally wrote:

Dear Craig

I'm sorry I made you angry but I have to stay true to my beliefs. I shouldn't have come; I realise that now. It's probably better if we don't meet again. Enjoy your breakfast.

Take care,

Amy

It seemed a very brief note as she looked over it, but what more could she say after all that had happened? She thought for a moment and then deciding there was nothing more to be said, she rinsed out her mug, leaving it on the draining board to dry and popped her yoghurt pot into the bin.

She left slowly, pausing only to return the keys to the table where she had found them. She didn't want to sneak a last look at Craig because she knew it would simply weaken her resolve. That chapter in her life was closed now forever.

Chapter Eight

Kate, assuming Amy had gone to London to see her mother, Jessica, enquired after her. "I was surprised you just left without a word about going," she said, a little hurt. "You know how fond I am of your mum. I might have gone with you if you'd asked me."

"It was just a brief overnight visit that's all," Amy said dismissively.

"Nothing wrong I hope?"

"No. I just fancied a change. Take my mind off things."

Kate nodded. She knew Amy was suffering for Craig and his situation.

"We'll probably hear from him soon," she said reassuringly. "He can't have much more time off work I imagine."

"No," Amy said, not wishing to be drawn to the subject any further. She had no desire to relive the events of the weekend and as time progressed she began to feel more and more dirty and sinful. Church seemed a closed book to her now, especially after reading Sammie's take on the subject in the final week:

Church, the topic of our final week. Plenty of explanation how to get connected through an introductory course to get you into membership but no real explanation of why you'd want to go down that route. Most of us value the freedom of having our Sundays to shop, enjoy a sport or be with the family. Church doesn't seem to be part of that life anymore. With numbers declining year on year, it's clear that for many people church is no longer relevant or any part of the average week.

How on earth, Amy pondered, could she make it part of her week anymore either, especially when she had betrayed the standards she had set for herself? Well, not fully betrayed them but wasn't there a passage in the bible that suggested that if you'd simply thought about doing something wrong, then, in reality, you had already committed that sin? She had done a lot more than thinking too. She'd gone halfway to actually committing the act and with someone who didn't even respect her. What had he said? That by going to his flat he had thought she was 'well up for it'. Was that really what he thought about her? Just a quick fling?

She made the excuse of illness as a reason for missing church the following day rather convincingly, she didn't look great having not slept well since she saw Craig. But she was completely unprepared for his phone call that evening.

"Amy, it's Craig. How are you?"

Stupid question. How did he think she was after the events of the Friday evening? She didn't answer.

"Umm look. I err ... I've been thinking about Friday night and I think I may have behaved rather badly. I've just got back to Charlesworth. Perhaps I can come round and explain things from my point of view, or even better, you could come here?"

Something in Amy suddenly snapped. Oh yes, she could see where he was coming from. Let's just take up from where we left off. Maybe she might just be 'up for it' this time. That wasn't even an option for her as a Christian; she had already gone a lot further than she ought to and lost some of her self-respect in the process.

"No, I don't think so," she said coldly. "I told you it's over and now the Alpha Course is over too we have no real need to see each other."

He was silent for a moment, perhaps considering his next move. Then surprisingly he suddenly said, "Please, Amy, please let's talk" in such a sad and beseeching tone it was all she could do to stick to her resolve.

Talk? There wouldn't be a whole lot of talk, she felt sure of that, only action and plenty of it.

"I think you've said enough," she said. "Have a good life and be happy." And she slammed down the phone before her resolve weakened.

Have a happy life she had said. How on earth was she to have a happy life? Amy put her head in her hands and wept and was still in that position crying her heart out when Kate found her on her return from church that evening. Amy had to tell Kate part of the story then, about going to see Craig as well as her mother and of giving him the card. She also said that they'd had a meal together and then she had left. She couldn't bring herself to tell Kate the rest of the story. She felt so ashamed.

Amy made an excuse to also miss the twenties and thirties evening the following Wednesday. She knew it was to be a ten pin bowling evening again and with memories of the last one still so fresh in her mind, she didn't feel she could face it.

"You can't still be ill, surely?" Kate said, peering at her rather suspiciously. "You usually enjoy ten pin bowling and our twenties and thirties socials and you have been at work all week. Is there something wrong?"

"No ... I," Amy was stalling for time. "I ... I really don't feel that great. Besides, I have an early start at work tomorrow, big day. I don't really want to go out late tonight."

The big day was in part true. Amy was going on a training course in IT for her company. It was the first that Brookes and Bradbury had sent her although she had now worked for them for over a year, but another girl had dropped out of the course due to family illness which Amy was sure was the only reason why she had been selected.

"Big day?" Kate asked, again suspiciously.

"Yes, you know. The IT training day. I told you about it at the local hotel."

"Ahh ... yes, I remember, but we won't be that late you know."

"No, really. I'd rather get my beauty sleep so that I won't embarrass myself tomorrow."

"Amy," Kate said in exasperation, finally giving up and grabbing her coat. "You never believe in yourself and never think anyone else does. I certainly do, Bill does and I was pretty sure that Craig did as well, no matter what you say."

"I told you it was all over between us," Amy said, her bottom lip starting to tremble and her eyes filling with tears.

"Amy, I'm sorry. Forgive me," Kate said immediately wrapping her arms around her. "I can see how much it hurts you. Maybe you do need some time and space to recover. I'll see you later." Giving her friend a quick kiss on the cheek, Kate picked up her handbag and went out to Rob who was waiting for her in his car.

Kate's words kept echoing through Amy's mind once Kate had gone. *Forgive me.* Kate's words certainly weren't unforgivable but would God ever forgive her? Could she forgive herself?

Amy wouldn't go to church with Kate the following Sunday either and when she also refused to go on the twenties and thirties movie evening the following Wednesday, Kate was keen to quiz her further.

"There's more to this last meeting with Craig than you've told me isn't there?" she asked with suspicion in her voice.

Amy sighed. The problem was her friend knew her only too well and it was difficult to hide much from the astute Kate.

"Well, yes, I suppose you might as well know all the sordid details. You'll probably find out sooner or later anyway."

"Sordid details?" Kate said suspiciously. "What do you mean?"

"Perhaps I should tell you later, you'll miss your film otherwise."

"Blow the film, friends are more important. I'll give Rob a ring and tell him I'm not coming and then make us both a cup of tea and you can tell me all about it."

After what seemed an age to Amy, now fretting badly, but was in fact only ten minutes, Kate returned with two steaming mugs of hot tea. She sat down beside Amy on the settee and encouraged her to talk. "I think it would be better for you to share your agony with someone else," she began. "I've seen you clearly suffering for the last week and a half and getting thinner and thinner."

"Kate," Amy began. "Don't be too shocked but I've behaved in a very bad way as a Christian."

Kate looked surprised. Amy could see this wasn't the confidence sharing she had expected.

"I feel ashamed and I don't think I'll ever be able to go back to church again and look people in the eye."

"For goodness sake, Amy, what on earth have you done?" Kate asked, looking a little afraid.

Amy felt now was the time to be completely straight with her friend. "You know when I said that I'd seen Craig the other week and had a meal with him and then left to stay with my mother?"

"Yes," Kate said impatiently.

"Well, that wasn't really true. I didn't see my mother at all. I stayed with Craig, slept at his sister's flat, only his sister wasn't there, only him."

Kate was silent for a moment, inwardly digesting the information, before she let out a sudden and incredulous, "You mean you slept with Craig?"

Then with realisation dawning she added, "You're not pregnant are you?"

"No. I slept there but not exactly with him or not quite anyway."

"What on earth do you mean?" It seemed to Kate as if her friend was talking in riddles. She put an arm around her and fell silent again for a few moments before saying, "What actually happened Amy?"

"Well, as you know, I went to the flat to deliver the card. I found Craig alone at his sister's flat. She was staying in France. He invited me in and the place was such a mess and he looked so sad and lost, I told myself it was my Christian duty to stay and look after him."

"Oh, Amy," Kate interjected, beginning to understand how things had happened.

"Anyway, I tidied up whilst he had a shower and changed. He was so thin and seemed to have survived on a largely liquid diet so we ordered a takeaway pizza between us. Then, after our meal, he started to tell me about the accident and how his father had been killed with a family friend, yet another of his many mistresses and how distressing it had all been for his mother and sister. I was comforting him and well ... one thing just led to another ... we got into a state of undress, but just in time I remembered that as a Christian I should only believe in sex in a committed marriage relationship and I told him as much. He was really angry with me. He's not a Christian and is used to bedding his women. I should have realised what would happen. I feel such a fool and we're not even on speaking terms now."

"But I thought he rang here the following night."

"He did and suggested we meet so that I could hear his side of the story."

"And you refused?"

"Of course I did. I'm sure he just wanted to carry on where we left off."

"You can't be sure of that."

"Oh, I think I am, knowing his track record."

Kate was thoughtful for a moment. "Maybe he is used to bedding women but who's to say you mightn't have meant a bit more than the others? In fact, I'm sure that Lisa told me he'd phoned in sick on that Monday after he rang you and I've also overhead some of the staff talking about the miserable long-faced Wilson at work."

"Don't try and make excuses for him," Amy said in frustration. "He's not a Christian and I should never have got involved with him. I know that now. It's just that there are so few decent Christian men at church and now if there were any I don't suppose they want a Jezebel like me."

Kate knew it was useless trying to reason with Amy or to suggest that she was being over-dramatic. Better to just comfort her for the meantime as Amy rocked herself backwards and forwards on the settee, sobbing as if her heart would break.

Suddenly she looked up through her tears and said, "You're so lucky to have Rob but how do you and Rob keep yourselves from going too far physically? The temptation can be really strong and even though you mean to marry you've still got to wait another year until Rob's passed his final lot of IT exams, haven't you?"

"Good question," Kate replied. "To be honest with great difficulty at times for both of us. But unlike Craig, he also believes that sex is best reserved for marriage to save people getting hurt."

"You're so lucky being in a relationship with someone who understands these things. God's rules about sex, marriage and relationships are wise, I realise that now. I wish I had paid a bit more attention to them and not listened to my heart."

"That's not always easy. Sometimes it's hard to control our feelings. I consider myself lucky finding Rob. I know that there wasn't a whole lot of choice for you and that's largely what attracted you to Craig."

Kate noticed her friend flinch just at the mention of his name. It was going to take Amy a while to get over him, she realised. "Why don't I ring Brian and see if you can make an appointment to talk with him about the matter?" she said suddenly, draining her cup and getting to her feet. "I'm sure he'll have some wisdom to share on the matter."

"Oh no," Amy said, horrified. "I couldn't possibly tell him. What would he think of me?"

"I'm sure you're not the first and won't be the last. Brian has been married to Carol for many years. He's sure to know all about sex and sexual matters."

"But I've never talked to him about such things. I think I'd die if I had to."

"If you go on moping and not eating the way that you are you'll die if you don't."

Amy had to admit the wisdom of Kate's words. She couldn't go on the way she had over the last week and a half. She felt she was living in a kind of hell. She nodded blankly and Kate went out to the kitchen to phone Brian. A few minutes later she was back.

"I spoke to Brian, caught him at home for once. Told him a little of how you felt that you had compromised yourself and your faith."

"You didn't go into what happened?" Amy asked nervously.

"No, of course not. That's for you to do. But Brian wants to speak to you. He said that he'd wondered why you'd been missing from church so much recently and would have followed it up himself if you hadn't gone again this Sunday. We made an appointment for tomorrow evening at eight pm."

"Oh dear," Amy said, now worried. "Well, I suppose he's got to know the worst about me some time."

Amy wasn't looking forward to the meeting the following evening but she knew deep down that she couldn't go on the way she was either.

Chapter Nine

Amy was feeling very apprehensive the following evening when Carol let her and Kate into the vicarage with a smile and a warm greeting, which she could only return with a nervous smile. As they were shown into the lounge where Brian was waiting for them on the settee, she felt even more nervous, especially as he stood up and shook both their hands warmly before beckoning them to sit down. They sat down in the two seats facing. Kate took the armchair, which Amy declined with a quick shake of her head, preferring the harder upright chair to keep her thoughts focused. After Carol had taken their orders for drinks and handed them out, she came and sat on the settee beside her husband.

"We've missed you at church recently, Amy," Brian said, "especially your lovely voice in the choir and your sunny smile."

"Yes, well …" Amy swallowed nervously. "I'm not sure what people would think of me if they knew what had happened."

"Never mind people, its God that matters. And don't forget that the bible is littered with characters who failed God in one way or another. God uses such people."

"But God seems distant at the moment and I feel I've not lived up to the standards I expected of myself."

"None of us do that," Brian said reassuringly.

"But do you believe in sex before marriage?" Amy asked, getting straight to the point.

"Well ..." Brian hesitated. "It's not the best thing, to be sure, better to get to know one another first, but sometimes there are temptations and things can get out of hand."

"They certainly can," Amy said miserably.

"Tell me about it, Amy, my dear," Brian replied, encouragingly.

"We didn't actually make love," Amy said nervously, "but we were alone together and went much further than we should have done before marriage, but I stopped him just in time." She blushed.

"I can't imagine he was too pleased with that," Brian said with a wry smile.

"No, he wasn't; he was livid. In fact, we're not seeing each other anymore. I know I should never have let the relationship go that far in the first place with him not being a Christian and that ... but it's hard sometimes when there are so few men in the church."

Brian sighed. "Yes, it's a real problem and I should imagine a source of some frustration to such a pretty young girl as you. I can well understand the attraction in a young, good looking man like Craig Wilson. But how did you get yourself in that situation Amy?"

"As you know, his parents, well actually it was only his father, were involved in a car accident. His father died along with another woman. Craig and I had begun to grow close over the Alpha weekend and so naturally I felt for him in his family tragedy. Then at the last Alpha evening, when Bill suggested sending a card to Craig and his sister, who were both staying at the sister's flat in London, I offered to post it. In truth, I had no intention of posting it. I was so desperate to see Craig again that I thought I would travel to London and take the card to the address on the envelope. I reasoned with myself that as it was the sister's flat and they were both present, then there would be no harm in the gesture. It might even demonstrate the care of the group. However, when I got there, I discovered that his sister, Annabel, had stayed over with her mother in France and Craig was alone in the flat. Of course I know I should have left the card with him at that point and gone, but I was so desperate to see him, to comfort him and the flat looked so untidy and he looked so sad, that I just couldn't help myself. I convinced myself it's the Christian thing to do to help others. But I'm afraid one thing just led to another ..."

Brian interrupted Amy at this point. "Which of course it would naturally do between two young people attracted to one another and alone together. Oh Amy, my dear, you put yourself and Craig in an impossible situation, one which couldn't have any other conclusion. I'm only amazed at your strength of character to being able to stop things going any further. That must have taken a lot of doing. He must respect you."

Amy shook her head wildly.

"I blame myself really," Brian said ruefully, "for giving too little teaching on sex and sexual matters in the church. It's not a good thing to spend lots of time alone with a member of the opposite sex, especially one you're very attracted to. I'm only surprised that if you'd been seeing quite a bit of him that nothing had happened sooner. Perhaps he thinks more of you than you realise."

"No, I don't think so," Amy said. She had begun to cry silently at this point and Kate placed a comforting arm around her shoulder. "I think he just wanted me for one thing only and not for friendship."

"Don't be too hard on him, my dear," Brian suggested kindly. "In his culture, bed is a natural progression to any relationship. It doesn't necessarily mean that he doesn't care. Did he try and contact you afterwards?"

"Well, yes he did," Amy said, slightly uncertainly, "but I said I wouldn't see him. I assumed he just wanted to take up where we left off."

"Not necessarily. But that aside, let's pray together. Jesus understands and doesn't judge sexual sin as any worse than any other. He knows our weaknesses and I believe he wants to forgive you, to give you a clean start. Then we'll pray about Craig and your relationship with him."

They all prayed together and as they prayed Amy felt as if a burden of sadness and misery had been removed from her. She still felt sad about Craig but not so completely in despair as when she believed that her faith had deserted her too.

"Now," Brian said. "We'll pray that Craig might come to know the Lord Jesus for himself."

"I don't think that'll ever happen," Amy responded miserably.

"Maybe or maybe not. But I think we should pray and believe that God can work in any heart. He may be much more open to faith now he has suffered such a terrible loss. Many people are."

Amy prayed fervently for Craig to come to know Jesus. She really wanted him to have faith. She didn't even care if he still didn't come back to her. She wanted faith for him for his sake because she knew how lonely he really was in his heart and how he pushed people away.

After this, she and Kate stood up to go. "Thank you for your time," Amy said quietly. "It has been really helpful."

"I only wish that I could have been there for you a little sooner. Helped you before you got involved with Craig and became so hurt," Brian said sadly. "But Carol and I will continue to pray for you and for Craig. There will be a way out of this situation, my dear, believe me." He patted her arm in a comforting gesture.

Amy did feel comforted. She also felt more peaceful about the situation than she had felt in a long time. God knew her heart and he knew Craig's. There must be some solution surely, even if it meant one or other of them moving out of the area.

Chapter Ten

Amy looked forward to going back to church that Sunday. She knew it was to be a special evangelistic service and that the choir would be taking an active role in the singing.

She was aware of a few people looking at her in a puzzled way, including Bill, no doubt questioning her few weeks of absence but was heartened by Brian's cheery smile and warm greeting.

Fred had chosen an interesting assortment of songs for the choir and congregation that day, many of which they hadn't sung for a while. But it was the final song which really moved Amy, the song based on psalm 121:

I lift my eyes up to the mountains, where does my help come from...O how I need you Lord, you are my only hope, you're my only prayer.

Amy had thought herself composed and able to deal with her feelings for Craig but this song proved her wrong. She began to cry quietly at first and then more noisily as Kate pulled her away from the choir and the stern frown of Fred Sharpe.

As Kate comforted her friend she was astonished to see Craig not only at the church but making his way to the front as the song ended and there was a call for prayer. What on earth was he doing here, was he still in pursuit of Amy? But then Kate realised he was crying too. She decided that it would be better to take Amy to the back of the church for a coffee and to avoid seeing Craig which might upset her even further. As they made their way to the back she glanced around to see Craig being comforted and prayed for by Brian and John, one of the young church worship leaders.

"I'm sorry, Kate," Amy said, screwing up the soggy tissue in her hand as Kate passed her a coffee when she had nearly stopped crying. "I thought I was over Craig but apparently not."

"You've got to give these things time," Kate said. She thought about telling her of Craig but then decided against it. It would be cruel to dash Amy's hopes again. It was too soon to know why Craig had been at church and gone up for prayer but in her heart, Kate started to feel more hopeful for her friend.

The two girls had arrived home and eaten a light lunch when the phone rang. It was Brian.

"Good singing today at church, Amy," he said. "How did you find it?"

How kind of him to ring and ask after her, she might as well be honest. "I was fine, really until the last song. I'm not quite over Craig yet as I thought."

There was a pause, and then Brian asked. "Did you see him at the church today, Amy?"

"No," Amy replied, surprised. "I wonder what he made of it."

"That's partly why I rang my dear. When I made the offer to pray with anyone, Craig was the first up the front accompanied by John, our young worship leader."

Amy then remembered how Craig had seemed to connect with John. She hardly knew him only that he was engaged to Nicky and that neither of them came to twenties and thirties that often, given that the socials often clashed with some of their worship practices.

There was another pause while Brian considered whether or not he should tell Amy how upset Craig had been but then decided against it. "Amy, my dear, Craig has made a commitment. It's early days yet but I believe it is a genuine commitment and that he really does want to join the church."

Amy could hardly take the news in. She was practically holding her breath and her face had become quite flushed. Kate noticed instantly and quickly grabbed a chair from nearby making Amy sit down.

"Are you alright, Amy?" Brian asked, worried by the somewhat tense silence.

"Ye ... ye ... yes ... I'm just trying to take in what you said. Do you think it's a genuine commitment?"

"Yes, I'm pretty sure. As I said to you, many people do turn to God when they have been through a bereavement especially one as tragic as Craig's. Amy, I've invited Craig round for a meal on Monday evening to give him a bible and talk a little more about what faith in God means and I wondered if you would like to join us?"

"I'm not sure he'd welcome my being there. Will he know I'm coming?"

"No to the second question. I wanted it to be a surprise and I think you may find that he will be very pleased to see you. Shall I take it that you'll come?"

"Yes, I will." Amy breathed in hard, her voice full of suppressed excitement. "What time?"

"Shall we say around seven?"

"Yes, see you then."

Amy put down the phone with a whoop of excitement. "What time is it now?" she asked Kate.

"About two pm," Kate said, puzzled. "Why?"

"In another five hours from now, tomorrow night, I'm going to see Craig again at Brian's house, although he doesn't know it and he's become a Christian, and Brian thinks he will be pleased to see me even though he doesn't know I'm coming and ..."

"Just slow down ... slow down," Kate said smiling widely. "I'll bring you a glass of water and you can start over again. I'm not really sure I follow the gist of this conversation."

Amy explained to Kate about Craig going up to the front at church and being prayed for by Brian and making a commitment.

"That's really fantastic Amy."

"Yes, isn't it? Brian said that people are often more open to God after they've suffered a bereavement," she said in a knowledgeable voice.

"Did Brian tell you anything else about Craig?" Kate asked carefully.

"No, only that he thought he would be pleased to see me and that my invite was to be a secret to him. Do you really think he will be pleased to see me?" Amy said, suddenly uncertain.

"I'm sure Brian wouldn't invite you unless he thought everything would be okay."

"Mmm ... yes." Amy looked thoughtful. "You know if Craig wants us just to be friends now so that he can concentrate on his relationship with God, I think I should be big enough to handle that, don't you think?"

"Well, for a while maybe," Kate said smiling in spite of herself.

"You think I can't handle my feelings for him, don't you?" Amy said, nettled. "Well, I can. If I genuinely believed it would be best for him and his faith I would even be prepared to move away from here and let him develop his own relationship with God."

Kate saw from Amy's determined expression that she was being completely serious. "I believe you would," she said, realising for perhaps the first time the depth of Amy's love for Craig.

Amy could hardly concentrate at work the next day and had to be told numerous things several times before she took them in. Jan looked at her in a puzzled way a few times and guessed from her nervousness and flushed expression that her distraction might have something to do with Craig but said nothing.

After a tea with Kate on her return from work, Amy decided she should ask her friend's advice in finding something suitable to wear. She tried on several dresses including a pink and white lace creation but then finally decided that her work trousers would be best.

"After all, it's a meeting of friends to celebrate his becoming a Christian and to concentrate on that. I don't want to be a distraction," she said, deciding on a grey tailored suit with a crisp white shirt. But Kate was amazed at how Amy could even make smart work attire appear sexy and interesting. Amy only allowed herself the luxury of a beautiful black and grey stone necklace with matching drop earrings to accentuate her outfit.

Eventually, the time came for her to leave. She had decided not to take the car but to walk to Brian's. She believed the walk and fresh air would help to calm and settle her nerves before she arrived. Carol opened the door and smiled, noticing Amy gazing nervously into the house in the expectation of seeing Craig.

"He's not here yet, Amy, after all, it's only 6.45."

Amy blushed. "I'm sorry Carol. I'm a little early aren't I? I could always go for another short walk around the corner for a few minutes."

"Don't talk nonsense. Come in, have a drink and settle yourself. You know you're always welcome here."

Amy was grateful to go into the vicarage and not to have to pace up and down any longer. She felt really nervous and apprehensive and was grateful for the glass of wine thrust into her hands.

Brian came in and gave her a warm reassuring hug. "He'll be here in a minute, don't worry Amy," he said as he saw her pale face. "Everything's going to be fine."

Amy had decided to make a dash to the toilet where she used the opportunity to send up a quick prayer to God:

Lord, help me not to make a fool of myself with Craig. Help me to stay calm and to keep the subject on you and not on me or anything more personal. It's his faith in you that's important not my feelings for him. Help me to remember that please Lord. Amen.

She was just coming back into the lounge when she heard the doorbell ring and her mouth went dry as her heart began to beat rather fast—was it him?

She heard Brian's warm greeting and then she heard Craig's reply. It was definitely him. Amy was torn between a desire to run away or to rush out and throw herself into his arms. And then he came into the room. Amy smiled nervously reflecting that the meeting was slightly easier for her as at least she knew he was coming. He didn't even know she was going to be there.

"A ... Amy," he stuttered.

She immediately noticed that he had turned slightly pale.

"Hello Craig," she said, with an attempt to smile brightly. "Congratulations on making a commitment. Brian has been telling me."

Craig looked awkwardly at his feet and there was a short pause before he said, "Thanks."

"Can I get you a drink, an apple juice, a beer or something?" Brian asked, interrupting the awkward silence.

"Mmm, yes please, a beer would be nice, thanks," Craig replied, but his eyes drifted onto Amy's face and remained there.

Brian and Carol both left on the excuse of having lots more preparations to do for the meal. They shut the door behind them leaving Craig and Amy alone.

Craig broke the silence first. "How have you been then?" as his eyes scanned her face as if to find the answer written there.

"To be honest, miserable. I've missed you terribly," Amy said. She felt frustrated with herself that these weren't the words she had wanted to say.

"Me too. Did you see me at church yesterday?"

"No, but Brian told me you were there and that you'd gone down to the front for prayer."

"Yeah. Crazy how it all happened really. I decided to go to St James first of all in the hope of seeing you; I'd really missed you, Amy."

Amy blushed. What did he mean by that? She said nothing, however, leaving him to continue his account.

"But before I even got near the church, a sense of compulsion drove me onwards as if I had no choice but to go. It was weird. Feeling rather uncomfortable and out of place, I sat in the back in the hope that no one would spot me. Then John did. You know John, one of the worship leaders?"

Amy nodded, willing him to continue.

"Well, he asked me if he could join me and reasoning that I'd rather have his company than that of some stranger, I agreed. I'd begun to feel a little more relaxed with him as we shared a few light-hearted comments but then the worship began. Honestly, Amy, it seemed as if all the songs had been written specifically for me, it was so strange. The one about the Father's love got me thinking about my own father again and this was followed by several others which all seemed to be about crying out to God, and him being the answer to our deepest needs. And then when Brian got up to speak, I could hardly believe it. It was in the self-same vein about the love of God, as if I hadn't heard enough of it by this time. It felt as if God was really trying to get my attention."

Amy smiled. God had heard her prayers for Craig it would seem.

Craig continued. "I felt so choked up but was equally adamant that I didn't want to drop my guard there in public especially in front of my mate John. But I was feeling totally overwhelmed by this stage and battling hard with my feelings. I asked God to stop baiting me. But instead, the sense of being loved just grew stronger and stronger within me, until we started singing that song after Brian's talk about needing God and him being our only hope. Then I just lost control and wept like a baby. The more I tried to stop myself the worse it got. I felt as if I were drowning."

"I'm so sorry," Amy said, "I didn't know." She lifted up her arms to comfort him and then thinking better of it, let them drop again beside her.

"Then, when Brian asked if anyone wanted to come to the front and make a commitment I just knew I had to go. It was as if God was talking just to me. John was great. I felt really embarrassed about being so out of control but he just seemed to take it all in his stride as if such things happened all the time. He just asked if I wanted him to go with me and not being able to talk at the time I just nodded. I didn't know what Brian would think of me breaking down in church like that either, but he didn't seem to think it anything out of the ordinary. Anyway, they both prayed for me and well, here I am."

"I'm so glad," Amy said. "I've been praying so hard for you but not just because of my feelings but because I knew you needed God, needed his love."

She blushed again wondering if she had said too much.

"God bless you, darling. I think you know me better than I know myself."

Darling, what did he mean by that? A bubble of hope grew inside Amy in spite of her promise to herself to remain impartial.

"I think it was that last song that really did it," he said ruefully. "The words got too close for comfort."

"I know exactly what you mean," she said. "It got to me too. In fact, so much so that Fred Sharpe glowered at me because my weeping was a distraction to him."

Craig smiled, and then quickly explained himself. "Oh, sweetheart, I'm sorry. I'm not smiling because you were upset but imagining the way in which you must have upset Fred's careful sense of equilibrium."

Amy smiled too, even more encouraged by his second use of an endearment.

"It was the first time I'd been to church in weeks too," she confided. "I felt embarrassed by what had happened between us and thought that God might not forgive me."

"And has He?" Craig asked, suddenly interested.

"Yes, I think so. I felt cut off from God after we ..." She hesitated. "Well, after we so nearly slept together. I felt that I'd lost my faith and couldn't find God anywhere. Brian said that God wanted to forgive me and that the bible is full of people that have failed."

"Gosh, Amy," he replied, running his hands through his hair. "I'm so sorry I put you through all that, I feel that I should take responsibility for any failure. I should never have touched you in that way but ..." His face was a mask of agony. "I couldn't help myself at the time. I feel so bad like I didn't respect you properly."

"No," Amy said and smiled weakly. "It was as much my fault as yours. I shouldn't have stayed alone with you at the flat but I felt sorry for you. I wanted to comfort you to be there for you, but Brian said that I put you and me in an impossible situation."

"Brian? Does he know about our lovemaking then?"

Amy blushed feeling a little tearful and about to lose Craig's respect and maybe his love. "Yes, well I had to tell him and Kate came with me. I felt I'd die if I didn't tell anyone."

"Oh, God." He passed his hands over his face as if coming to terms with the situation.

Amy began to cry quietly. "I'm so sorry, Craig. I know what a private person you are. You probably hate me more than ever now, even more than you hated me for stopping our lovemaking."

"Amy, I could never hate you, darling. I love you with all my heart. Come here." He held out his arms to her and she ran into them as they hugged one another tightly.

When they finally pulled apart he said, "It was the frustration of wanting you that made me angry that night. I wanted you so badly. Now it's only the shock of having my life exposed to others that I find so hard to bear. It makes me feel vulnerable, a little bit like the crying thing. But I think I'm going to have to be bold enough to open up my life to others now, especially to you and God. Bear with me darling, it's not easy for me. As you once said, I haven't allowed people close to me for some time."

He'd remembered her words at the pub that night after the Alpha Course evening all those weeks ago, storing up her words in his heart. She felt so loved in that moment and as she looked up into his eyes she saw that love shining clearly out of them.

"Oh, Craig, "she uttered and before she could say any more she felt the strength of his lips bearing down on her, as he pulled her closer and closer to him. The kiss seemed to go on forever and they were both panting and breathless as he released her.

"I thought at the time that I was just another woman to you, a challenge to get into bed like all the others," she said once she'd regained her breath.

"But I tried to tell you on Alpha weekend that you were different."

She nodded, remembering that instance which she had dismissed at the time as another flirtatious statement.

"I feel ashamed at my past treatment of women now," he said bitterly. "When my father died in his car along with that other woman I hated him for the grief he'd caused my mother and Annabel and then I saw that I was becoming like him, a mirror image of the man I hated."

"But you didn't really hate him, did you?" Amy asked gently putting her arms around him.

"No, I guess not, although I could never please him, even though he'd passed on one of his old Jags to me when he bought the saloon," he said thoughtfully.

Amy nodded. This answered an important question she still had in her mind.

"That aside, Amy, darling, I realised what a womaniser I was also becoming, exactly like him. But being truthful, you were never one of a list. With you, it was always different. That first time when we oh so nearly made love together was a bit of a first for me too. It wasn't mere sex like all the other times, it really was making love and if you're prepared to believe I might become the man you could love enough to wait for, until marriage, well ... I'd like to be that man."

"I only said that I was still waiting for the man I could love that night because I thought that I was just another woman to you and I didn't want you to see how much you'd hurt me."

"Amy, are you saying what I think you are? I can never apologise enough to you. I never wanted to hurt you." He looked so anguished that Amy gently laid a finger on his lips.

"Ssshh, it's okay now. I love you, Craig. I've loved you since that first moment of our meeting at the Alpha supper."

"I think that did it for me too," he said smiling. "So, what's your answer? You can't keep a man in suspense, especially one who loves you so much."

"Answer to what?" Amy said, puzzled.

He cleared his throat. "I was asking you, probably not that well, if you'd do me the honour of marrying me."

Amy thought she'd never seen Craig looking quite so awkward or unsure of himself and couldn't resist a slight jibe.

"I'm surprised to see the journalist and writer for once struggling for words," she said with a coquettish smile.

Craig groaned. "You certainly know how to keep a man in suspense. I'm not finding this easy, but from now on I'd like to share all of myself with you and God. Please marry me Amy and put me out of my misery."

"Oh yes please, "she replied happily. "Yes please, my darling Craig."

They kissed again passionately and this time, Amy broke away with a sudden thought.

"When are we going to get married then?"

"As soon as we can if I've got anything to do with it," he said, "because I'm going to need an awful lot of cold showers before then."

Catching his meaning Amy blushed and smiled. "I think I might just need a few myself."

Craig laughed as Amy continued on with the thought. "Are you really prepared to wait for me then?"

"I would wait for you forever my darling," Craig responded instantly, catching her up in his arms again and dropping kisses all over her face.

At that moment, they both heard the door opening and jumped apart quickly like two guilty teenagers. Brian and Carol came back into the room with Craig's beer and smiled beneficently at the two youngsters struggling to keep apart, as they announced that dinner was ready.

"Great, I'm famished," Craig said honestly.

"You certainly both look a lot happier and in need of a good feed," Brian said, smiling broadly.

"Yes and we'll be in need of your services as a minister to marry us soon," Craig replied, also smiling hard.

Carol and Brian hugged Amy warmly and shook Craig's hand. "Well done both of you. It was worth holding the dinner back for such a result. This was what we both hoped and prayed for."

And, laughing and smiling together, Brian and Carol led the way into the dining room with Craig and Amy following behind, their arms entwined around one another.

About the Author

Under her pen name of Sheila Donald for fiction, Sheila Johnson is a UK based writer with over ten years experience as a successful freelance journalist. Alpha Male is her first published book. When Sheila is not writing, she enjoys singing and listening to music, films, the theatre, cooking, swimming and Formula One racing.

A further selection of Sheila's articles can be found on her website and she can also be followed on twitter and linkedin:

http://www.journojohnson.blogspot.com
http://www.twitter.com/journojohnson
http://uk.linkedin.com/in/journojohnson

Made in the USA
Charleston, SC
20 June 2016